ORIGINS

BOOK 3

CHILD OF ATLANTIS

CATALYST

PERRY COVINGTON

THINK KINGS PUBLISHING

ISBN-13: 978-0-9972496-0-6
ISBN-10: 0-9972496-0-9

First American edition, February 2016

FOR MY DAD,
WHO DOES NOT SETTLE FOR WHAT IS,
BUT STRIVES FOR WHAT COULD BE.

CONTENTS

PROLOGUE

ONE

Professor Auggie - 8

TWO

Heart of the City - 14

THREE

Church of the Chosen - 29

FOUR

Cabin Fever - 40

FIVE

Summoned - 46

SIX

Breaking News - 51

SEVEN

Reunion - 54

EIGHT

Victory or Death - 67

NINE

The Gathering - 72

TEN

Road Trip - 84

ELEVEN

7 Ninjas of Iga - 90

TWELVE

Cover Charge - 99

THIRTEEN

Mother Earth - 107

FOURTEEN

Trials of Kratos - 116

FIFTEEN

Cyber Warfare - 120

SIXTEEN

Round One, Fight - 128

SEVENTEEN

Bad News - 137

EIGHTEEN

Round Two, Fight - 141

NINETEEN

Seeds of Doubt - 146

TWENTY

Round Three, Fight - 148

TWENTY-ONE

Wrench's New Toy - 153

TWENTY-TWO

Final Round, Fight - 158

TWENTY-THREE

The Drums of War - 162

TWENTY-FOUR

Deploy - 172

TWENTY-FIVE

Calm Before the Storm - 175

TWENTY-SIX

Blood Thicker Than Water - 184

TWENTY-SEVEN

Attack on Lemuria - 187

TWENTY-EIGHT

Beacon News - 192

TWENTY-NINE

To War - 194

THIRTY

Launch - 200

THIRTY-ONE

Ground Battle - 205

THIRTY-TWO

The Snake in the Grass - 209

THIRTY-THREE

Look to the East - 212

THIRTY-FOUR

Battle of Gods - 219

THIRTY-FIVE

Eruption - 224

THIRTY-SIX

Fatal Blow - 227

EPILOGUE

> *Augmented Uniform Guard 1496 now online.*

> *Accessing file > 1125.*

> *Subject > Origins.*

Now uploading...

"There is no greater schism than a house divided."

"The culling was nigh to complete the cycle, but those who rebelled stood fast. The Founder's will, be done."

"In the darkness, the light shall be born again, marching forward until the holy task is complete. United, the People are, but in the face of such horrors, their mettle will be found wanting."

-Shi'Tal Codex, The Great Cycle 2: 6-12

PROLOGUE

Plato checked his watch again. The timing had to be absolutely perfect. A single slip-up would cost him weeks of planning. He called up his HUD and checked the environmental read-out. The arctic weather wreaked havoc on his instrumentation, but the M.A.R.S. suit that he and his six-person team were wearing was more than capable of handling the extreme weather.

Plato, and his team, hid silently in a depression of a security wall, right outside of the building they were observing. The time they had spent in the cold for this reconnaissance was at an end. Now, it was time for execution. Plato looked at his watch, one last time, before activating the communication system on his suit.

"We are cleared hot," Plato whispered. The humor of the phrase was not lost on him as he smirked and wiped away the snow that was building up on his face shield from the blizzard that raged on.

Immediately, Plato saw six green lights flash once, indicating his team had received his transmission and were good to go. Radio discipline was crucial on a mission like this. Plato had tried for months to find this enemy base, to no avail, but the Seeing Stone that Alastriona gave him a few weeks prior had made this mission finally possible.

Plato turned and jumped up twenty feet, the M.A.R.S. suit and his own Atlantean abilities making the leap effortless. He gracefully

1

landed on top of the wall, hardly making any noise at all. His suit's infiltration grid was active and the camouflage made him nearly invisible. Plato looked to his left and he barely made out the figures perched next to him; their figures wavered like a mirage. If it weren't for his HUD indicating where his comrades were, he probably would not be able to see them without really concentrating.

The team looked below and saw all of the guards walking away from the wall. Several yards in the distance, more guards emerged from the building, ready to relieve the outgoing guards from duty.

Shift change, Plato thought. He projected that thought telepathically to his teammates and, once again, green lights flashed. This was their moment. A small window of opportunity while the shift change took place. A moment of distraction.

The seven-person team leapt again, this time from the top of the wall to the top of the roof of the building, a forty-foot gap, but merely a small hop for the extraordinary abilities of the Atlantean people. As soon as the team landed cat-like on the roof, they all fell to the deck onto their stomachs. Plato stole a glance upward and saw the security cameras sweep across where they had just been standing. The camera rotated away and Plato hopped to his feet and ghosted across the roof, his team close behind.

Plato made a beeline for a shaft that issued bulbous clouds of steam. He knew that shaft was going to be their best bet for infiltration. Plato crouched by the vent and opened up his HUD. He accessed a link with a satellite overhead and a streaming video of them on the roof. His M.A.R.S. suit had a neural connection to his body that enabled a heads-up display to appear in Plato's field of vision. The streaming video began to play in the corner of his simulated display. Plato switched modes on the powerful camera, located on the satellite that was floating miles above them in space, and he saw an infrared view of the roof they were on. Plato could see the faint outline forms of he and his team as minimal heat escaped their suits. Directly below them, Plato saw three figures that shown brightly in red and orange on the infrared camera.

Targets acquired, Plato pushed to his team. *One guard. Silva, you're up.*

Four members of the team pulled out small metallic devices and held them over the screws that fastened the lid of the vent. They switched on the devices and an invisible magnetic field went to work on the screws, twirling them out with ease. Once the vent was removed, the one Plato called Silva tugged on a rappel rope that was securely fastened around his torso. He gave Plato a quick salute, then dove headfirst into the vent. The four who had removed the vent cover took up the slack of the rappel rope and pulled back, slowing Silva's descent down the shaft.

Remember, Silva, disable only, Plato pushed.

Plato was one of the most powerful telepaths of the Atlantean people and he could easily sense Silva's annoyance at Plato's orders. Plato couldn't rightly blame him. Weeks ago, the Fallen had ousted many of the agents assigned to the Citadel, the city Plato and his team called home. The Fallen somehow found many of the occupied safe houses of the Order of Light, and mercilessly killed the agents there. Plato was beyond anger and grief, but he had a role to play. He was their leader. Without sound judgment, he could easily lead them to ruin.

Plato patched into Silva's video feed. A small display appeared on the right side of his field of vision. At first, all Plato could see was darkness and the occasional wisp of steam that engulfed the agent. Silva looked down and saw a dim light slowly increasing in intensity. The agents holding the rope tightened their grips, slowing Silva's descent until he softly landed on the vent separating the room below him and the shaft that led outside.

Contact, Silva pushed to Plato.

Plato breathed deeply, trying to mask his anxiety.

Carefully, Silva. Carefully.

No worries, boss.

Silva pressed a button on his right gauntlet and a small compartment, the size of a coin, opened up. Out of it flew what looked to the casual observer as a small household fly. In actuality, the fly was a highly sophisticated nanotech drone used for surveillance. The drone's camera automatically linked with Silva's heads-up display and, in turn, with Plato's. A warped video stream played across their HUDs as Silva directed the drone to fly down through the vent.

Once through, the drone landed on the ceiling, right next to the vent. In a room the size of the one that Plato and his team were infiltrating, static observation was the best practice.

Less movement the better, Plato thought privately.

The fly drone repositioned itself so its camera could get a better look at the targets. A man wearing black armor was intently staring at a bank of monitors. The drone zoomed in. On the guard's screen, videos on YouTube played, as the man chuckled to himself softly.

Government work, Silva mused.

Stay sharp, Plato responded. *Pan the camera. Are the packages secured?*

The drone shifted and the video feed revealed two large hab-units, each holding a person lying unconscious. The man and woman looked gaunt, but the readouts on the hab-units showed that their vitals were steady.

Plato let out a breath that he was unconsciously holding.

Is that?... Silva began to think.

It is, Plato responded. *Deploy.*

Silva took control of the drone and launched it, from the ceiling, directly at the distracted guard. The drone was nearly silent as it flew through the air. Silva pressed another button that armed the stinger in the drone. Once the drone made contact, the stinger would plunge into the man's neck and the sleeping agent within the stinger would render the guard unconscious.

The drone was a few feet from making the injection when the man suddenly spun around in his seat. He swatted at the drone. Silva tried to correct course, but the man's quick reaction to the drone's presence was too much for the little drone to handle. The back of the guard's hand smacked the drone right out of the air, and the video feed that Silva and Plato were watching showed the room spinning until the drone crashed into the far wall, cutting the feed entirely.

"Weird," the guard said to himself, as he stood up to go examine the fly. "I thought I heard a buzzing." He walked over to the drone, crossing right under the vent that Silva was standing on.

Orders, boss?

Plan B. Still try and subdue.

Silva smirked to himself. *Do my best, boss.*

Silva carefully lifted the vent, activated his invisibility camouflage, and jumped quietly down to the floor. The guard looked at the fly closely and noticed it sparking slightly.

"What in the hell?" he murmured.

PROLOGUE

"That was my favorite drone," Silva whispered behind the guard.

In one movement, the guard spun around and drew his gun, searching for a target. Silva was still cloaked, but he sidestepped out of the way of the barrel of the gun, just to be safe.

"Show yourself," the guard demanded. He reached for the device in his ear to call for backup, but before he could do so, a jolt of energy blazed through his neck and he was instantly knocked out.

"Night-night," Silva said, as he uncloaked and put away his stun baton.

All clear down here, boss.

Plato jumped down the shaft without the aid of ropes. He was powerful enough to control his descent with his telekinesis with ease. He landed on the ground floor as softly as if he were stepping out of an elevator. He surveyed his surroundings.

"Was all the chatter necessary, Silva?" Plato asked quietly.

"That drone *was* my favorite, boss," Silva responded with a smile.

Plato walked over to the hab-unit controls and surveyed the read-outs. "They are weak, but alive. Thank the Founder. Signal the team and prep for evac."

"Yes, sir."

Silva walked back to the vent and issued orders to the team above. Plato's fingers danced across the controls and soon the curved door on the hab-unit that was holding the woman hissed. Plato entered the same commands for the second unit, then rushed over to the woman as she woke. Plato took her hand gently.

"Lara, it's ok. I'm here. You and Jack are going to be fine," he whispered.

Lara's eyes fluttered and looked around wildly until they settled on Plato's face. Plato smiled warmly.

"I've been looking for you."

Lara smiled weakly. "Hi, Dad."

CHAPTER ONE

PROFESSOR AUGGIE

Max and Alana floated weightlessly under the surface of the ocean. Max could almost hear his own heartbeat pounding in his chest. Below them, the glow of the eyes illuminated more of the creature that was coming. Max could barely make out its head and, at the distance he was at, he could tell the creature was overwhelmingly titanic. Already, the width of its head was at least four times as large as the length of Vincini's ship.

The beast opened its mouth and a bright blue light emanated from it. The same blue energy winked on, down the spine of the creature, and Max could finally appreciate the sheer size of this monster. It was larger than anything he had ever seen before. The beast let out its deep roar and, again, it shook Max and Alana.

The creature moved like a snake through the water, its head shifting back and forth, and it was fast approaching. It was the master of the ocean, a weapon in which there would be no rebuttal.

Max...

The Leviathan.

Then it was gone. The lights that played across the megalithic body of the Leviathan beneath them winked out. Instead, up above them, at the surface of the ocean, a steady white light shone. Max looked to the source of the light as a beacon. He didn't know what was creating the magnificent glow, but he was drawn to it like a moth to a flame. He whipped his arms and legs trying to swim to the surface while pulling Alana up with him. His lungs burned and his muscles protested from the effort.

Wait, this doesn't make any sense, Max thought. *Alana, why isn't my aqualung working?*

Alana didn't respond. Max looked back and his confusion turned to horror. Alana hung lifeless in the murky water. The light from above played across her pale face and he saw that she wasn't wearing her aqualung. Her mouth hung limply open and Max had to shut his eyes, realization slamming into him like a train. A great pain welled in his chest. He wanted to scream out into the depths of the black ocean, but he had no breath left in his lungs. Max went into survival mode, kicking and pulling himself towards the surface. He didn't let go of Alana… he couldn't. He had to get her to the surface. He would Recall his CPR training. He could save her. He had to.

As Max swam towards the surface, he saw other people in the water. Ghostly figures floating in the abyss. His friends.

No, no, no, no. Please!

The light from above was eclipsed suddenly. Max looked up and saw another figure floating directly above him. He activated his suit lights to see who it was. A few feet above him, the face of his childhood friend stared blankly back at him. Wayland's eyes were milky white, his face bloated, and his body was still. Wayland. Dead.

No!

Max exploded. The energy of his Atlantean abilities blazing out in a sphere, flash boiled the water around him. The blue energy formed a great ball of power as Max released everything stored within his body.

Max woke with a start, the sound of his own yelling pulling him from his dream. He sat up and looked bleary-eyed at the people sitting next to him. He was in a makeshift classroom and an elderly gentleman stood at the front of the room. The professor looked aghast for a moment, then his skin began to ripple. His body shimmered out of existence and in its place stood a gangly robot with a book in his hand.

"Are you alright, Maximus Hunter?" the robot asked.

"Wha… what happened, Auggie?" Max asked, as he rubbed his eyes.

"I believe you fell asleep during my dissertation on the effects the great flood had on surrounding continental borders."

Alana reached out and put a hand on Max's shoulder from the desk she sat in behind him. "Max… you alright?"

Max turned around and looked intently at her.

Same dream, Max?

Max nodded.

"Oh, come off it, you two," Osiris shouted from his desk in the back of the room. "It's bad enough we have to go to school while we wait here in this godforsaken volcano you Lemurians call home," he said, as he pointed at Ronin and Charlie, "but, your little telepathic conversations," he said, looking at Max and Alana, "are annoying as hell."

"Max is having visions," Alana spat at Osiris. "I'm worried about him. You two are mates, aren't you? Shouldn't you be worried, too?" she accused.

"Max is a big boy, love. Oh, and B-T-W, he's also the Key. I think he can take care of himself."

"Maybe we all just need to blow off a little steam, just chill for a bit," Wayland offered.

"Stay out of it, mate," Osiris said quickly.

Alana took a deep breath. "No, Wayland is right. I think we all need to, what did you say Wayland, 'chill' for a bit." She turned to Auggie. "Apologies, Auggie. I know Plato wanted us to continue our studies while we are waiting for him to return from his trip, but we've only arrived a few days ago from our last mission. Let's call it a day."

"As you wish, Alana," Auggie said.

"An excellent development," Ronin said, as he stood and offered his hand to Charlotte. "The princess and I will return to the castle. I've a mind to get some training in. Would any of you care to join me?"

"Yeah, I'll go," Wayland said eagerly. "Someone has to teach me to not get beat up all the time."

Ronin thumped Wayland on the back as he walked over. "Wonderful. It will be my honor to assist in your road to greatness. What say you, Osiris?"

"No, I think I'll go for a walk. Stretch me legs for a bit. I'll see you all back at the flat for supper," Osiris said, as he walked out of the classroom.

Alana, annoyed, watched him go.

"Just let him get some air, Alana," Max said. "We have been through a lot. Oz is just dealing. Being cooped up doesn't help either."

Alana nodded. "I know how he feels. When I learned Simon was in league with the Fallen, I didn't know how to feel. Relief, anger, frustration. All of the above."

"Do you think what Simon said about Oz's dad is true? You think he's alive and working for Malus?" Charlotte asked, as she slung her bag over her shoulder.

"It's possible," Alana said, as she sifted through her thoughts. "It would certainly explain how the Fallen were able to bypass our security systems at the Battle of the Citadel. Primus probably gave them access.

"It is a hard pill to swallow," Ronin said. "Battle Master Primus is one of the most celebrated warriors of our age. The victories he claimed at the Trials of Kratos alone are legendary. He is an honorable man."

"Sometimes wanting power is stronger than wanting honor," Wayland chimed in.

Ronin slapped him on the shoulder again. "Very wise my overly large friend. Come, we waste our breath on politics. Let us spend it on the field of battle instead." Ronin and Charlotte regally walked out with Wayland and Auggie in tow.

"We're just practicing, right?" Wayland called, as he tried to catch up with Ronin. "Auggie, you have to keep an eye on that guy. He might try to take my head off."

"I have your back, best-friend-Wayland."

Max smirked. *I love those guys.*

"Yes," Alana said as she finished gathering her stuff. "Me, too."

"So… what should we do for the afternoon?" Max asked awkwardly.

"Let's tour the city. It is my understanding that the Collective of Lemuria is quite wondrous."

"Cool, let's do it. I could use some wonder in my life," Max said.

CHAPTER TWO

HEART OF THE CITY

Max and Alana left the building where their pseudo-classes were being held and made their way into the city proper of Lemuria. The city was ablaze with life. If Max had to compare, he would say the city closely resembled the hustle and bustle of New York. There was, of course, a large castle at one end of the sprawling metropolis, which looked completely out of place, but still… like New York. Max mentally shrugged. Not much surprised him these days.

Everywhere Max looked, people were rushing by, busy with their lives. It looked like an ordinary city. Max looked up and saw the opening of the dormant volcano they were in.

Mt. Rainier.

"Amazing, is it not?"

"Yeah, it really is. But, I guess Atlanteans like to 'go big' as opposed to 'going home'," Max said absentmindedly.

"I'm sorry, you lost me," Alana smiled.

"Something my dad used to always say," Max mused. "He was always saying crazy stuff like, 'Go big or go home, Son.' "

Max rubbed the back of his neck.

"Don't worry, Max. Master Plato is out there, right now,

looking for your parents. He said he had a good lead, remember? Elder Plato is a man of his word."

"I'm sure he is Alana, but I just don't see why we couldn't go with him. I'm the Key, right? You'd think that would buy me some say in rescuing my parents."

"I know it's frustrating sitting here, feeling helpless. We must trust in Elder Plato."

"Easier said than done," Max murmured.

"Come on, let's go look at the mountain core. The Lemurian's call it the Heart of the City."

Max and Alana walked down the main thoroughfare of the city. As they progressed, the tall buildings that occupied the center of the city became sparse.

"I thought we were going to the heart of the city?"

"Just because it's called the heart, doesn't mean it's in the center of the city," Alana said, as she checked a palms-up display. The thin bracelet she wore was a device that could display a small hologram, accessing various apps whenever you turned your palm upward. Currently, Alana was looking at a map of the city. "Here we are," she said, pointing at a red marker. "Here is where we need to go." She tapped an icon and the map was linked to her neural network. She could now see overlaid directions within her actual field of view. "Max, do you want access to the A.R. map?"

"Augmented Reality makes me motion sick. I'll just follow you, if it's all the same?"

Alana smirked. "Come on. I'll go slow so your tummy doesn't get an oww-ee."

"Ha, ha. You're so funny."

They walked further out from the main body of the city. The only light that was provided was the soft glow of street lamps and the dim light from the opening of the volcano several hundred feet above.

"How long have the Lemurians called this place home?" Max asked, as he craned his neck to look up at the opening of the volcano.

"Thousands of years," Alana answered. "They have lived here ever since the schism between the Order and the Fallen."

"So, they just didn't want to get caught up in all the fighting?"

"Partly. The Lemurians actually left a few years before the fighting broke out. They were a group of people who were deeply devout to the Atlantean religious practices. They believed in the teachings of the Shi'tal Codex, so much so that they declared that those who did not practice the holy teachings of the Codex were heretics. Even the Cleric Guild believed the Lemurians to be too radical. So, the Lemurians left and made their home here. Nowadays, the Lemurians have eased up on their religious vigor, but there are some who still hold to the old rhetoric."

"They moved to a volcano? Real smart move."

"That's why the mountain core is so interesting. The Lemurians have built a geo-thermal reactor there to harness the power of the volcano. They actually temper the volcano and use its potential destructive force for more productive means."

"Alana, we're going to a power plant? Really? I thought you said we were going to see something *wondrous*," he said, as he made quotation marks in the air with his fingers.

"A city powered by volcanic activity isn't wondrous enough for you?" Alana asked incredulously. "Stop whining. I'm trying to culture and educate you."

"I thought you also said that was enough school for today?"

"You're such a baby. Come on, we're here."

Up ahead, a large metallic building, that seemed to be embedded in the side stone of the mountain, came into view. The building seemed to be neglected. Rust adorned the walls and the paint was peeling. Several large pipes protruded from the roof and snaked their way up the face of the stonewall towards the volcano's opening.

"That is the reactor plant," Alana said, tapping icons on her heads-up view of the map.

"Doesn't look like much," Max said. "I wonder how many people work here?"

They walked to the front gate of the building. It was an unimpressive chain-link fence that had a red warning sign.

"Authorized Personnel Only," Max read aloud. "Well, looks like we came all this way for nothing."

"We can jump this fence easily enough," Alana said, as she mentally did calculations in her head.

Max grasped her by her shoulders and looked intently into her eyes. "Who are you and what have you done to my rule-following Alana?"

"Oh, come on," Alana laughed, as she shrugged Max's hands off of her. "Look, there is a buzzer on the gate. Maybe someone who is working can let us in. If not, then a quick look around won't hurt anything."

"That's it. We can't hang out anymore. I'm a bad influence on you."

Alana raised a mocking eyebrow as she walked over to the call box on the gate. She pressed it and immediately a camera shot up from the ground from a hidden compartment. Alana and Max took a quick step back.

The camera floated for several seconds, turning back and forth from Max to Alana.

"Hi," a voice called through a speaker on the camera.

"Um, hello," Alana said unsure.

"What's up?" the camera asked.

"Nada, what's up with you?" Max said amused.

"Chillin'," the voice said.

"Uh, do you work here, at the plant?" Alana asked, still confused.

"Yup, sure do. Cool gig if you ask me," the camera said happily.

"Are you some kind of A.I.," Alana said.

"Nah, just the regular kind of intelligence."

"Dude, are you a computer or an automaton, or something like that?" Max asked beginning to get frustrated.

"Nope, just an engineer."

"Ok… may we come and tour the facility?" Alana asked.

"Really?" the voice asked surprised.

"Yes, really," Max said quickly.

"Sure," the voice said.

They both stood awkwardly for a moment. The camera continued to float, shifting its attention back and forth from Max to Alana.

"Like, right now," Max said quickly.

"Oh, right, come on in," the voice said, as the buzzard sounded on the gate and they walked in.

The camera dove below ground again and Max and Alana walked cautiously to the steel door of the building. When they were within a few feet, a red warning light came on above the door. It reminded Max of the lights on top of police cars. A loud buzzard sounded and the steel door opened slowly. As it did, Max and Alana saw a young man standing in front of them. He didn't look much older than they were.

"Hi," he said.

It was the same chipper voice from the camera.

"Hi," Max and Alana said together.

"You work here?" Alana asked, with a hint of disbelief in her voice.

"Yup."

"Who else works here?" Max asked, as he looked around the interior of the door.

"Just me and the ladies," the man said.

"Ladies?" Alana asked.

"Well, they're all A.U.G. units repurposed to help me run the reactor."

"Dude, you're like a teenager. You run the reactor?" Max asked skeptically.

"Yup. Seventeen to be exact; if you're going by earth years, of course."

"Um... most folks do," Max said.

"The name's Wrench," the boy said. "Well, my name is actually Bartholomew W. Braxis III, but most of my friends call me Wrench."

"Um, ok. Got lots of friends, do you?"

Alana elbowed Max in the side.

"Well, I guess just the ladies call me that, but they're all pretty cool. Come on, I'll show you around!"

Wrench walked away, Max and Alana trailing behind.

"Ladies? He's crazy," Max mouthed silently.

Alana just shrugged and resigned herself to their unlikely tour guide.

They walked down a non-descript hall for a minute, which led to an elevator. The elevator opened as Wrench approached. Inside, blue lights glowed softly.

Wrench stepped in and turned around to face Max and Alana. "Come on in."

"Where does this elevator go?" Max asked.

"Down, of course," Wrench responded.

"To what?" Alana asked.

"To the reactor. This top building is just a front for all the really cool stuff down below."

Max looked at Alana and shrugged.

They both entered the elevator and the doors closed behind them. The elevator began to descend.

Max laughed quietly to himself.

"What?" Alana said, with a smirk on her face.

"Just remembering the first time you brought me down to the Citadel. The elevator, the blue lights. Just funny."

"If I remember correctly, you were unconscious for most of that elevator ride," Alana smiled.

"Yeah, up until the part you said that I was cute."

"You were awake for that?!" Alana asked, embarrassed.

Max laughed. "Sorry. I was trying to figure out where I was before you knew I was awake."

"Unbelievable," Alana said, as she punched Max's arm.

Max laughed again and then stopped abruptly when he noticed Wrench laughing heartily as well.

"Oh, good times," Wrench said, as he wiped a tear from his eye.

Max stared at him for a moment. "You're not around people much, are you?"

"How'd you know?" Wrench said, astonished. "This guy is psychic," Wrench said to Alana, as he jerked his thumb towards Max.

"Yes, we're Atlantean. We all are, to some degree. But, I don't think Max was reading your mind," Alana said, as she sidestepped away from Wrench.

"Right, sorry. I spent most of my time with the Earthborn. I forget about the Atlantean thing sometimes. Actually, I forget a lot of things... at least I think I do. Um... I spend most of my time alone. I was younger than the other M.I.T. students, so they didn't want to play D&D with me very often," Wrench said, looking to the ground, his shoulders drooping.

Max and Alana looked at each other.

I feel terrible now.

Yeah, me too, Alana pushed back.

The elevator bell dinged and immediately Wrench's head popped up.

"Hey look, we're here," he said jovially, as he walked out of the elevator.

Max raised his eyebrows to Alana, as he pointed a finger to the exiting Wrench. "Crazy," he mouthed.

She held up a hand as she walked out.

They walked into an area the size of a warehouse. On the outer walls was a strip of glass, approximately six feet tall, that bisected the walls and stretched across most of the perimeter of the area. A faint orange-red glow emanated from the windows.

"Come on," Wrench called from further into the warehouse.

The cavernous room was full of tables laden with various bits of technology and tools. In the center of the room were several large grey machines. They had legs and arms and, in the torso, a large cockpit. Max walked up to one that stood approximately ten-feet tall. On one of the forearms, *S.P.R.T.N.* was stenciled in black lettering.

"What the...?" Max began to say.

Wrench popped his head out from behind the leg of the machine, making Max jump.

"Pretty cool, right!?"

Alana strode up from behind Max.

"What are they, Wrench?" she asked.

"This bad boy is one of my S.P.R.T.N. units. A squadron of these would be an effective way to make up for the Collective's lack of

22

security," Wrench said proudly, as he patted a gun turret. "Designed and built them myself… with the help of the ladies, of course."

"Spartans, like from 300?" Max asked with a smirk on his face. "Good movie."

"Right!?"

"Wait, what does S.P.R.T.N. actually mean, and what did you mean 'lack of security?'" Alana asked, surveying the weaponry on the machine.

"Single Piloted Reconnaissance and Tactical Neuro-Suit," Wrench said. "They are meant for one person to pilot it. Its neuro-link and the bank of cameras across the suit allow you to see several things at the same time. Just a few of these things can hold back dozens of targets at once. Lemuria doesn't have a standing army. All we have are a few dozen security personnel, which the kick-ass Ronin commands. He's so cool. He's the First Knight of the Realm. How awesome is that!? I wanted to show him the S.P.R.T.N.s, but he's busy fighting bad dudes and stuff."

He thinks Ronin is cool? That proves it. Totally nutballs.

Stop, Alana admonished.

"They are very impressive, Wrench," Alana said graciously.

"Yeah…" Wrench said, as he stared up at his creation, lost in thought.

Again, several silent moments passed, awkwardly, and Max was forced to speak up.

"Wrench, the reactor."

"Huh, oh right, the reactor. Totally why you're here. Got it. Uh… this way."

They walked to the wide windows and immediately Max realized where the orange and red glow was coming from. Several meters below them was a river of lava. It steamed and roiled as it made contact with the edges of rock, hardening and softening almost instantly. The lava seemed to be alive.

"Whoa, that is actual lava right outside this window," Max said astonished. He touched the window with a finger. It was completely cool. "How…"

"That is Shatter Glass, trademark pending," Wrench said. "It's cool, right? Oh, ha, see what I did there?"

Max rolled his eyes. "Shatter Glass? Does it break easily or something?"

"No, just the opposite. It doesn't shatter at all. Well, I don't think it does. A few more tests," Wrench said frenetically.

"I don't get it," Alana said quizzically. "Why call it Shatter Glass then?"

"It's ironic. Get it?"

"No," Max and Alana said in unison.

Wrench shrugged. "Cool. Cool, cool, cool."

"So… the geo-thermal reactor," Alana said, trying to keep the conversation going.

"Yes," Wrench responded with a smile on his face.

"Um… how does it work?"

"Work? Oh right. Yeah, it totally works."

"How?" Max said, through gritted teeth, his annoyance barely contained.

"Good question," Wrench said, as if he were teaching a class. "It's simple really. We recover the heat generated from the magma and use it to power turbines, heat water, heat homes, and so on and so forth. We can also control the magma flow from valves embedded in the volcanic vents and fissures throughout the mountain. When pressure builds up, we release it into a collection unit and convert that to useable energy as well. It's all very efficient and it also keeps the volcano from goin'… you know… boom," Wrench said with a nervous laugh.

"Yeah, but Rainier has erupted before, right?" Max asked, Recalling his history lessons.

"Yup, back in the late 1800s," Wrench said. "The pressure valves weren't that great back in the day."

"Amazing," Alana said. "And, you monitor it all yourself? Quite a feat, Wrench."

"Well, me and the ladies," Wrench said.

"Where are these ladies you keep talking about?" Max asked.

"Oh, how rude of me," Wrench said. "Ladies, come meet our guests."

Throughout the warehouse, clangs and whirring could be heard. The cacophony of noise was jarring. Max instinctively reached for his sword, Excalibur, but it wasn't there.

"Whose idea was it to leave our swords back at the flat?" Max asked on his guard.

Alana stood very still, ready for anything.

Around the corner came several automatons that had miniature tracks for legs and spindly arms. They looked like very old versions of what Auggie was. Their diminutive size and large dulcet eyes made them look cartoonish and almost cute.

Max and Alana relaxed a little.

"This is Jenn, Eleanor, Daisy, and the shy one there in the back is Mykel," Wrench said. "They're my best friends!"

"Greetings, Wrench. Greetings, Wrench's friends," the robots said in unison.

"Aaand, I'm officially weirded out. Time to go, Alana," Max said under his breath.

Agreed.

"Well, Wrench, it was lovely visiting with you and your, um, friends, but we best be off," Alana said.

"Oh, no, don't go. There is this one really cool thing I gotta show you. You'll love it! It's been here forever. Buried deep under us, in a massive chamber!"

"I'm sure we would," Alana said, "but, we really must be…"

At that moment, the comm-link on Alana's bracelet began to chime. "Terribly sorry," Alana said. "I should take this."

Wrench nodded emphatically.

Alana tapped the bracelet then turned her palm upward. A hologram of Wayland appeared. He looked distraught.

"Is it on, Aug?" Wayland asked, as he checked the camera, giving Alana, Max, and Wrench a good view of the interior of his nose. "Alana, you there?"

"I'm here, Wayland. Back away from Auggie's camera."

Wayland backed up and saw Alana's image. "Oh, hey, cool. This thing works. Sweet, Auggie," Wayland said, as he gave a thumbs up to Auggie. "It's like Star Wars! Auggie, watch this. Help me, Alana, you're our only hope," Wayland said, as he laughed and bumped fists with Auggie.

Alana shook her head and smiled. She still didn't quite understand Wayland's friendship with Auggie.

"So, hey everyone," Wayland continued.

"What's up?" Max said, as he moved closer to the projection.

"Max, what's up, my brother? Should have known you two would be together," he said, as he winked.

"She can see you, you know that right?" Max said, embarrassed.

"Oh, right, sorry. So, anyway... You guys better get down to the church in the middle of the city. Looks like Oz is about to put a beating on a few of the church goers here."

"They are called the Acolytes from the Church of the Chosen," Auggie said, off camera.

"Right, Acolytes," Wayland said. "Thanks, buddy."

"You're very welcome, best-friend-Way…"

"Would you two knock it off?" Max said. "Oz needs help?"

"Yup."

"Like right now, right now?"

"Yup. Right now, right now. I don't know if Ronin can talk him down. Actually, now that I think of it, Ronin actually might instigate the fight. That guy loves a good fight. He's so weird. It might get ugly."

"Yesss," Max said excitedly.

"Dude, did you hear me, right?" Wayland asked confused. "I said it could get ugly… Aug, are you sure it's working right?" Wayland said, as he looked away from the camera.

"We'll be right there," Max said, as he tapped the icon to end the video call. "So sorry, Wrench, we have to go. Order of Light business. You understand?"

"It's cool. I'll show you the thing next time you come by," Wrench said, a little crestfallen.

"Um, yup," Max said, as he pulled Alana away towards the exit.

"So sorry," Alana called. "See you soon, Wrench." She genuinely felt bad for leaving him all alone.

Max and Alana got back to the elevator and the doors shut as they began their ascent.

"Whew, that was close. Good thing Oz is in a fight," Max said, as he looked up at the display indicating the floors.

Alana elbowed him in the ribs.

"Ow, what did I say?"

CHAPTER THREE

CHURCH OF THE CHOSEN

Using the comm-link bracelet, Alana was able to GPS-locate Auggie. At full speed, Alana and Max were able to run to the Church of the Chosen within a few minutes. As they approached the church, Max saw a small crowd formed in front of the massive building's front steps. With Max in tow, Alana weaved through the crowd to get to the small clearing in the middle. In the crowd, there were people dressed in white robes yelling at the individuals in the center of the group. The crowd of people was dense, forcing Max to push several people out of his way. The bodies of the crowd seemed to ebb and flow like a tide, centering on the conflict like an eye of a storm. Max and Alana broke through the last line of people and what they saw made the hair on the back of Max's neck stand on end.

Four robed church members, carrying swords, surrounded Osiris. Their robes were tattered and soiled. Streaks of blood painted across the once pristine fabric. Osiris stood in the middle of the attackers, his own swords in each hand. Osiris's shirt had been ripped off in the battle, fresh wounds adorning his chest and arms.

"Come on, you bloody nutters! You issued the challenge. It's time to collect," Osiris said with a maniacal grin.

Max knew that grin. It was the grin of a guy who was about to do some serious damage. The four church members circled Osiris, probing, looking for an opening. Osiris stood still, tracking each person with his eyes.

Alana spotted Ronin and Charlotte standing a few feet away and made her way to them. Max followed. Ronin was cheering loudly for Osiris, like he was at a WWE match, while Charlotte looked on silently, beneath the hood she was wearing to hide her royal status.

"What in the Founder's name is going on?" Alana asked Charlotte.

"Oz insulted one of the Acolytes," Charlotte said.

"And?"

"That's it," Ronin said with a wide grin. "Now he battles!"

"The two of you aren't making any sense," Alana said.

Wayland, who stood at least a head above everyone else, made his way through the crowd towards them. Auggie was close behind. "Hey guys!"

Max looked up at him. "What happened, Way?"

"Oh man, you guys should have seen it. We were all walking together. Oz was about to break away from us to go to the apartment when he saw one of these Acolyte people. I'm not sure what he said, but the next thing we know, three more Acolytes were running out of the church carrying swords."

"The Acolytes issued a legitimate challenge, under the laws of the Collective of Lemuria," Auggie chimed in. "Osiris accepted."

"But Oz is not a Lemurian," Alana protested.

"The law applies to outsiders," Auggie countered.

"Well, I'm not going to stand by and watch Oz take on four people by himself," Max said indignantly. He began to walk towards the fight, but Alana grabbed him by the arm.

"Max, you can't just go around fighting everyone," Alana said earnestly.

"Why not? Oz is," Wayland said, pointing at Osiris and his attackers.

Alana rounded on Wayland, anger flashing in her eyes. "Max is the Key. He has responsibilities he is beholden to. He can't afford to offend different factions of the Atlantean people, especially when our allies are so few."

"Well, when you put it like that," Wayland said crestfallen.

"I'm not going to fight them, Alana. I'm just going to try and talk some sense into them," Max said, trying to sound as benevolent as possible.

Alana arched an eyebrow. "Fine, but tread carefully, Max."

"Yes, Mom," Max said, over his shoulder as he walked to the middle of the circle.

Osiris spotted him and smiled broadly. "Now you gits are in for it," he snarled at his opponents. "Did I forget to mention that the Key and I are mates?"

Max held his hands out to his sides, palms facing out, in an attempt to look like he meant no harm. "Look, everyone, I'm sure this whole thing is just a huge misunderstanding. There's no reason…"

"Nah, no mistake, mate," Osiris interjected. "I insulted their religion, the nutters that they are, and they challenged me to a dual. I gladly accepted. I've been bored out of my mind in this dingy volcano."

"Oz, you're not helping," Max whispered out of the corner of his mouth.

A tall man stepped from the crowd and approached them. He wore the robes of the Acolytes, save for a large blue stripe that ran down the center of his robes. The lights from the street reflected on his polished baldhead. His movements were smooth and deliberate, like a snake weaving through tall grass.

That is the High Magus, Alana pushed to Max. *The leader of the Church of the Chosen. Careful Max.*

Got it.

"Welcome, Key of the Altantean people. You are welcome here, Savai, make no mistake," the tall man said, a little too grandiose for Max's taste. "I am Judias, High Magus of the Church of the Chosen, fourth son of Venator the Ever Seeing, humbly at your service." Judias bowed his head slightly towards Max.

"Um, thanks," Max said awkwardly. "Nice to meet you. I'm Max, the... um Key, from uh, San Diego."

Max heard Wayland snort from laughter behind him. Max could feel his face grow warm from embarrassment.

"My friend didn't mean any offense, I'm sure." Max tossed a withering glance to Osiris. "We don't want to cause any further trouble. We'll just go and forget..."

"Ah, Savai, I am greatly saddened and embarrassed. You see, your friend cannot leave. It is written, as you well know, in the Great Codex, that 'he so whomever bring discourse to the Founder's will, shall be stricken down'. The Founder's will, be done."

32

The group of Acolytes that surrounded them echoed Judias. "Founder's will, be done."

The way they spoke in one voice gave Max the creeps. "Right... so it is written," Max said a little unconvincingly. "But, I was hoping we could just overlook this little transgression and, you know, maybe hug it out or something."

Judias looked scandalized. "Savai, do you wish for us to go against the Founder's written and holy word? As Speaker, we look to you for divine guidance on all matters concerning the Founder. Is the Founder's will to forsake the Great Codex and all its teachings?"

He's trying to trap you, Alana warned.

Max's anger flared. He didn't like being pushed into a corner. "No one is saying that you should forsake anything. I just think that your people might have misunderstood my friend. We aren't from around here. Your customs are different from what Oz might be used to."

"He blasphemed," an Acolyte yelled, as she pointed the sword she was carrying towards Osiris. "We must have justice."

"JUSTICE!" the crowd of Acolytes yelled.

Judias raised his hands, and instantly the crowd quieted. "Peace, brothers and sisters, peace. We will have justice." Judias turned to Max. "What say you, Savai, will you deny the Faithful the justice they deserve according to the Founder? Blessed be his name."

"The Founder is a 'she'," Osiris said.

Max closed his eyes in quiet frustration.

"Again, he blasphemes," Judias spat.

"No, he's just messing around..."

33

"Enough!" Judias yelled. "I can see the rumors about the Key are true. You are not of the Faithful. You have been tainted by the outside world!" He raised a hand and brought it down, and Osiris's opponents resumed their attack.

Max jumped into the air and summersaulted towards Osiris. As he did, Osiris threw one of his swords into the air and Max caught it mid-air before landing nimbly behind Osiris. They were now back-to-back facing the Acolytes.

"Enough with the drama, baldy. No one touches Oz." Max said.

"The Key has interfered with proceedings of the challenge. His life is forfeit!" Judias yelled. The Acolytes from the crowd all converged on Max and Osiris, drawing weapons from beneath their robes.

Using her telekinesis, Alana waved both hands out, like she was doing the breast-stroke and the crowd parted, tumbling over one another from Alana's power. She drew her sword and charged down the cleared path. Auggie, Wayland, Ronin, and Charlotte were close on her heels.

"You want to attack the Key, you must come through me," Alana shouted. The Acolytes around her stepped back, fear in their eyes. The ferocity in Alana's voice even scared Max a little.

Charlotte threw back the hood she was wearing and her crown shown brightly under the lights of the city. "Cease this nonsense, at once!" she commanded.

A hush fell over the crowd. Many of the non-Acolytes in the crowd dropped to one knee in reverence. Even some of the Acolytes bowed, but hesitated when the rest of their brethren did not.

"Princess Charlotte, my, my, this is quite the day," Judias said, the disdain obvious in his voice. "What brings you to our little place of worship? Have you and your betrothed finally succumbed to the true faith of the Chosen?"

"You know I'm a devout follower of the Codex. I do not adhere to your dogma. I am the crowned Princess of the Collective of Lemuria. I follow the teachings of my own accord. You would do well to know your place, Magus," Charlotte spat.

Judias bowed his head slightly. "Such is your right, Your Highness." He said the last word like he was spitting poison from his mouth. "But, even you cannot ignore that a Lemurian law has been broken. A challenge was issued. Osiris Pendragon accepted. Should we go to the queen to moderate this dispute?"

"Who issued this challenge?" Charlotte retorted.

"I did, Your Majesty," said an Acolyte who had a cut running across his chest.

"Repeat your challenge verbatim," Charlotte commanded.

The Acolyte looked to Judias for instruction.

"Do not turn to the Magus when your Princess is addressing you," Ronin roared, as he drew his own sword.

The Acolyte paled at the sight of Ronin, the most celebrated warrior of the Lemurian people.

Charlotte placed a hand on Ronin's shoulder to calm him. "Magus, do you and your Acolytes not recognize the crown as the sovereign ruler of the Collective? Am I to believe that you have defected from our warm embrace?"

Judias looked as if he were about to have a heart attack. His entire head turned beet red. "No, Your Majesty," he said with forced restrain. "Of course not. Answer the princess, Brother Xavier."

The Acolyte named Xavier bowed quickly. He glanced sidelong at Ronin who still held his sword aloft. "Your Majesty, I said to Osiris Pendragon that for the crimes of blasphemy against the Church of the Chosen, that I challenged him to a dual to the death."

Charlotte nodded her head contemplatively. "Those were your exact words?"

"Yes, Your Majesty."

"You stated that 'you' challenged Osiris?

"Yes, Your Majesty."

"Yet, before me, I see three of your compatriots standing by your side to battle against Osiris. Why is that Xavier?"

"Pendragon is formidable. Reinforcements were needed to…"

"Reinforcements…" Charlotte said over Xavier. "As it stands, the only one I see as breaking our laws is you." She raised an accusatory finger at Xavier. "You issued the challenge. Osiris accepted. Then you broke that solemn covenant when you called for reinforcements, did you not?"

"Well.. yes, but…"

"Then, it is by our laws that I must bring you to account for your transgression," Charlotte said.

She is absolutely brilliant. Alana pushed to Max.

Max was too enthralled with the proceeding to respond.

"What do you think a fitting punishment would be for your Acolyte, High Magus? I ask out of respect for your position as the leader of the Church of the Chosen, such a reputable and venerable establishment that it is," she said mockingly.

Judias stood fuming, his rage slowly boiling to the surface. "I'm sure fair and wise judgment will be given by Your Majesty."

"Yes," Charlotte said, lazily as she traced her finger down the metal of Ronin's sword. "I am fair and wise, aren't I?"

Ronin grinned slightly.

Charlotte sighed dramatically. "Well, I suppose I could let Osiris finish what he started, and judging by that nasty wound across your chest, Xavier, he would make short work of you."

Osiris twirled his sword in anticipation.

"Of course, it is the Founder's will that the people of Atlantis practice 'patience and understanding towards our brethren'. The Founder's will, be done."

"The Founder's will, be done," the group echoed quietly.

Now she's quoting scripture! Alana pushed excitedly. *She will make a fine queen some day.*

Max nodded emphatically. *So glad she's on our side.*

Judias snapped. "You cannot quote scripture of the Great Codex to me…"

Ronin moved like lightning. He dashed towards the Magus, his sword hissing through the air, its tip halted centimeters from Judias's nose. "Tread carefully, Magus," Ronin whispered. "Do not presume to tell her Majesty what she can and cannot do."

"Peace Ronin. I'm sure the High Magus is emotional from all of this," Charlotte said, as she waived her hand around.

Ronin sheathed his sword in one deft movement, but stayed rooted to his spot, staring daggers at the Magus.

"Today, we will all be patient and understanding," Charlotte said, as she turned to address the crowd. "Osiris has been warned about our laws and our ways and, from this day forth, will abide by them. The Collective of Lemuria welcomes all those who are tolerant of each other, and embraces the differences we all have. Let all present stand witness; Osiris has been educated. Xavier will be forgiven for breaking our laws, even though he and the rest of the Church are well versed. We cannot let our emotions rule us. We are a people that remain humble. Hubris will only lead to anger and suffering. Depart this place, my people, and go in peace. Let us all reflect what we have learned here today."

The crowd began to disperse. Osiris sheathed his sword.

"Well, boys and girls, thanks for the workout," he said, as he smiled and bowed his head slightly.

The four Acolytes scowled as they put away their own weapons. Judias gathered them and spoke to each of them in hushed tones.

Max turned and shoved the hilt of the sword he was holding into Osiris's chest. "You're lucky Charlie was here to save your butt."

Osiris laughed. "What? We could have taken them."

"Not the point, Oz, and you know it."

"You both are lucky," Alana said from behind them. "I told you not to fight anyone, Max."

Max turned quickly. "They started it, Alana. They were going to rush Oz. I had to do something."

"You need to take lessons on tact from Charlotte. At least she knows how to control a crowd."

"Well, thank you," Charlotte said, as she and Ronin approached the group.

"Yeah, you were totally badass," Wayland said, as he and Auggie joined them. "That Magus guy was like, 'You cannot, blah blah blah,' then Ronin was like, 'Nuh-uh, fool,' then Charlie was like, 'Boo-yah, I'm a princess.'"

Ronin smiled widely. "I enjoy your storytelling, my giant friend."

They all laughed.

"Enjoy your little victory," Judias said to them from a few feet away. They all turned to face him. "Now that your mob is out of earshot, I can say freely that you have offended the Founder with your faithless ways. There will be a reckoning for the those who are not Chosen."

"Is it your wish that I dispose of him, Your Majesty?" Ronin inquired, as his fist curled around the hilt of his sword.

"Stay your blade, my love. The High Magus knows I would not condone such wanton violence in our fair city."

Judias scoffed. "Your fair city is full of faithless. But, we will show them the path to enlightenment. Mark my words."

Judias turned and walked back to the church, his robe billowing behind him.

"That dude is cra cra," Wayland said.

"Indeed, best-friend-Wayland. Cra cra, for sure," Auggie chimed in.

CHAPTER FOUR

CABIN FEVER

Wayland fell onto one of the couches of the flat that he, Max, Alana, and Auggie were assigned to. Osiris sat with Alana on a bench while she tended to the wounds he suffered from the fight against the Acolytes. Max, Charlotte, and Ronin sat on various couches and chairs throughout the sitting room while Auggie moved quickly about the kitchen preparing a meal.

The flat was metropolitan in nature. The dark wooden floors were highly polished and reflective while the walls were all painted neutral colors. Recessed lighting gave the space an ethereal feel. The place was fully stocked with food, clothes, and every type of entertainment. To Max, it felt like a prison, designed to keep them distracted and placated.

"Ow," Osiris winced.

"Relax, you big baby. It's just as well as you deserve," Alana admonished, as she applied ointment on a large gash on Osiris's shoulder. "You'll heal quickly, but according to Auggie's analysis of the wound, I believe the blades were laced with some kind of compound that slows Atlantean regeneration. Hence, the need for the ointment."

"Acolyte sadists. How many times do I have to apologize?

They were asking for it. I didn't start it," Osiris countered. "I was minding me own business when those gits came at me. I had to defend myself."

"By making fun of their religion?" Max responded with a smile.

"No reason I couldn't have a little fun."

"Pay no attention to those Acolytes," Ronin said, as he removed his torso armor to make adjustments. "They are poor excuses for Lemurians. They hide behind their religion to further their own political agendas. They have no honor."

"Then why do you guys let them hang out in the city?" Wayland asked. "Just kick them out already."

"They have never openly opposed the Collective," Charlotte said. "I have long appealed to my mother for their expulsion, but that would go against our own laws of acceptance. The Collective does not discriminate against its citizens so long as they abide by our laws and uphold our anonymity."

"It is true," Ronin chimed in. "The Collective is home to Atlantean, Caster, Hunter, and even to some of the more civilized Cryptids."

"Hence the name, the *Collective* of Lemuria," Auggie said, as he chopped vegetables.

"Nailed it, buddy," Wayland said. "Toss me a carrot to munch on, will ya?"

Auggie threw a freshly peeled carrot to Wayland and he caught it in his mouth. Wayland and Auggie both raised their arms in triumph.

"I'm telling you, Alana, we can't be cooped up here forever," Max sighed. "It's no wonder that Oz is out picking fights."

"Didn't start it," Osiris said casually as he turned on the television.

"I think we're just going a little stir crazy," Max said, ignoring Osiris.

"Be that as it may, we must be good guests. Charlotte and the queen are not obligated to rescue us, nurse us, and play host to us."

Alana bowed her head slightly in thanks at Charlotte, who returned the gesture.

"Yeah, explain all that to me again," Wayland said. "How did the rescue go down? I was a little passed out from blood loss when that poser, Vincini, stabbed me with a freaking Tablet of Fate."

"Destiny," Max corrected.

"Whatever. I got stabbed, it hurt, and I passed out."

"Ah… such grand adventures we have had together," Ronin mused, as he examined his sword.

Wayland stared at Ronin for a moment. "You're a strange dude."

"As I've said. Plato acquired the Seeing Stone," Alana said, as she finished applying a bandage to Osiris. "He was able to scry our location using its powers."

"Scry?" Wayland asked.

"Think of it as a mystical GPS locator. The Seeing Stone is composed of fragments from the Great Crystal. The stone is engineered to enhance one's telepathic ability, allowing an adept user to *see* things all across the world," Alana said.

"Whoa. Just like in *Lord Of The Rings,*" Wayland said.

"Fiction often mimics real life," Charlotte replied. "It is said that in every legend there lies a grain of truth."

"So, Plato found us on Atlantean Google Maps. Then what?" Wayland asked.

"Then my mother dispatched a rescue team to retrieve us," Charlotte answered.

"What about the Leviathan?" Osiris asked, as he inspected his bandages. "That thing was right on us."

"I believe it was a matter of proximity," Auggie said. His back was turned to the group as he stir-fried vegetables in a wok. His head turned 180 degrees to address them. "The Leviathan functions when both Tablets are activated. A system that Wayland the Smith and Da Vinci created as a failsafe for its activation. One Tablet was embedded in best-friend-Wayland's chest while the other was in the possession of the Fallen as they flew away in their drop-ship. Once the other Tablet was out of range, the Leviathan simply shut off."

"So we were saved by a bad signal?" Max asked. "Thank goodness the Wi-Fi is crappy out in the middle of the ocean."

"Indeed," Auggie agreed. "I don't believe we were in any real danger, at any rate. The Leviathan was merely surfacing. From the information I've been able to gather from my database, the Leviathan requires a pilot. Also, there was a flux in the electromagnetic spectrum in the approximate area we were located. My sensors picked up the anomaly when we were aboard Da Vinci's yacht. It might explain why the Tablets had a diminished ability to communicate with the Leviathan. The flux occurred when the vessel entered the region that is commonly known as the Bermuda Triangle."

"Aug… do you mean it was aliens, bro?" Wayland asked in awe.

"Way," Max said exasperated.

"What? It could be, Max. You don't know, man. I've seen *Ancient Aliens* on the History Channel. That stuff is legit."

"Every Atlantean knows the Triangle has some old buried tech down there," Osiris said. "It was probably the actual Leviathan causing the interference."

"But why would the Leviathan create interference against itself?" Max asked.

"Exactly. Aliens, bro."

"Way, you can't seriously…" Max's comm-bracelet suddenly blazed to life, buzzing and emitting a soft chime. Charlotte's bracelet did the same. Max and Charlotte both turned their palm upward, and a small holographic image of Queen Alastriona winked on.

Osiris turned the television off and they all looked at the glowing figure of the queen.

"Good evening, venerable Key, and greetings to you, my beloved daughter," Alastriona said, as she bowed her head slightly.

"Your Majesty," Max said.

"Hello, mother."

"I require the presence of the two of you here at the palace immediately. Only the two of you," Alastriona said sternly.

Ronin stood and walked over to Charlotte. He bowed deeply and addressed Alastriona. "Your Majesty, I humbly request your permission to accompany the Princess. Her protection is my number one priority."

"Your request is noted and denied, First Knight of the Realm. I appreciate your diligence, but I need to speak with the Princess and the Key alone. I have sent an armored transport to gather them because I know the consternation my summons will cause you, my valiant Knight. Rest easy. They will be safe."

Ronin remained in a bowed position. "As my queen wishes, so it shall be done."

Charlotte could hear the worry in Ronin's voice. She stroked his cheek reassuringly. "Do not fret, my darling. I will be safe," she said gently.

Ronin glanced up slightly and smiled.

"Your Majesty, I don't like to keep things from my friends. Do you mind if we all come?" Max asked.

"I appreciate your bond with your friends, but I must insist. All will be revealed soon enough."

Max looked to Alana. She nodded. "Alright," Max said. "We'll be outside waiting for the transport, Your Majesty."

"It is already outside," Alastriona said. "Make haste, time is a fickle friend."

The hologram blinked out.

CHAPTER FIVE

SUMMONED

Max and Charlotte entered the automated transport. Max glanced down at the base of the vehicle and noticed that there weren't any tires. Anti-gravity technology was still something he wasn't quite used to. The vehicle was sleek and the majority of its body was transparent. As soon as Max and Charlotte sat down, the transparent walls darkened and the vehicle began to move. The interior was very spacious and posh. Since there wasn't an area where a steering wheel was needed, the majority of the space was dedicated to comfort and entertainment.

Charlotte touched a finger to one of the curved walls. "Window," she said softly. Immediately, the darkened glass became transparent on the panel she was touching. Outside, Max could see the Lemurians on the city sidewalks going about their business.

"Pretty cool," Max said, as he touched the panel closest to him. "Window."

"These surfaces will respond to a variety of commands. You can bring up video feeds, watch movies, play games, and even…" She touched the transparent panel again. "Window, open." The viewing port dissolved and the air from outside rushed in. "… enjoy the breeze," she finished.

"Wow. That is amazing. How…"

"It's molecular manipulation technology," Charlotte said.

"I'm going to pretend I know what you're talking about," Max said, as he stared out onto the metropolis.

Charlotte laughed softly as she sat back in her seat to enjoy the view as well. It was evening and the lights of the city were vibrant. The multitude of colors from the different businesses and buildings cast a rainbow of light across everything. The babble of the pedestrians filled the air. People laughed, argued, called for cabs… all the trappings of a normal bustling city. Scents from the restaurants wafted through their windows and Max breathed in deeply.

"It's easy to forget about how different all of this is compared to the outside world," Max said, almost to himself.

"I can understand how hard this must be for you to accept. We have existed here, much like our compatriots in the Citadel, for thousands of years. The Earthborn have no idea of the hidden world we have created here," Charlotte said.

"Everything I've been taught about history is wrong. Everything I know about the world is wrong."

"Not necessarily. What you have been taught isn't wrong, simply a piece to a much larger puzzle. Earthborn history is also our history. The fates of our two peoples are intertwined. That is what we teach here in Lemuria. While different, we are much more connected than we could ever imagine."

"Why is Lemuria split from the rest of the Atlantean population?" Max asked.

"We aren't split," Charlotte laughed. "We just don't believe in meddling in the affairs of others. We believe acceptance and respect is the best measure of a good neighbor. The Fallen want to rule, the Order wants to usher the Earthborn into the next stage of their existence. Both sides want to exert their will over the Earthborn. The Collective merely coexists. We believe that eventually our fates will come to a head with the Earthborn, naturally of their own accord. Until that day, we live peacefully and quietly, as it is written in the Great Codex."

"I guess that sounds pretty cool." Max sat quiet for a moment, and then he frowned and turned to Charlotte. "So why are those Acolytes so extreme? Don't they follow the same religion you do?"

Charlotte sighed. "They claim they do. But, it is as you said, they are extremists. At its purist, raw form, most religions are peaceful and preach many of the same ideologies. Most of it boils down to just being good to each other. A noble endeavor, to be sure."

"I wouldn't use the word *noble* to describe the Acolytes," Max said.

"Neither would I," Charlotte agreed. "They have taken the scriptures of Shi'tal Codex and twisted them to serve their own purposes. They believe that the Atlantean race will soon be called back to the Founder, and we will be transported to paradise. Lemurians believe in achieving a peaceful 'eternity though faith', but we achieve that through the understanding of our world and all its inhabitants. The Acolytes are separatists at their core. In their eyes, only the *Chosen* can achieve that eternity. Any involvement with anything that does not focus on this ideal is considered sacrilegious to the Church of the Chosen."

"That's just crazy."

"My mother always said, 'Religion is at its best when people are not involved,' " Charlotte said, as she was momentarily lost in a memory.

"People do have a tendency to screw things up," Max agreed.

Max looked out of the window and noticed the buildings and crowds were becoming less prominent.

"We are entering the inner sanctuary of the palace grounds," Charlotte said. "We will be at the castle soon."

Max watched as the technologically festooned streets of the city gave way to open courtyards and cobblestone streets. It was almost like traveling back in time. "The palace is kind of... old school, huh?"

"We make a concerted effort to maintain our traditions by upholding the lifestyle of our forebears," Charlotte said, as she surveyed her subjects. "It helps us stay grounded. This castle was once the home of King Arthur himself. Each stone was transported here, piece by piece, during the Exodus."

A man on horseback bowed deeply as the vehicle passed him.

"It's like being at Medieval Times."

"Is that a place?" Charlotte asked.

"Yeah, I'll take you and Ronin one day. You guys will love it."

A group of armed guards flanked the large portcullis that acted as a barrier between the palace and the rest of the grounds. Max saw that they carried weapons that were both futuristic and ancient.

"I heard someone say that Lemuria doesn't have much of an army. Is that true?"

"It is. We do not believe in having a standing army. We have peacekeepers for local affairs, but since we make it a point not to get involved with the wars of the outside world, we have no need for an army."

Max suddenly realized that his presence there, in the Collective of Lemuria, meant that the Lemurians were now involved. They had chosen a side. "Charlotte, I don't think I've ever really thanked you and your mom for helping us, for helping me. I know what this means for you and your people."

Charlotte smiled. "There comes a time when a person must make a stand. Remember when I told you that the fate of the Earthborn are intertwined with that of the Atlanteans?"

"Yeah."

"Well, the Fallen have forced our hand. We can no longer wait for destiny to take its course naturally. The Fallen have interrupted fate's plan. The queen has decided that in order to attain balance once again, we must aid the Key in his efforts."

"Yeah, well, I'm really grateful. I'm lucky to have met you and Ronin. You guys are good friends."

Charlotte smiled broadly. "Come, my friend. We have arrived."

CHAPTER SIX

BREAKING NEWS

Osiris flipped through the channels on the holo-display. Ronin stood by the window of the flat, staring out into the city. Wayland stuffed his face with delicious stir-fry as Auggie watched him eat. Alana sat on a tatami mat meditating silently.

As Osiris flipped channels, he came across a news broadcast, midway through its report. All eyes turned to the holo-display.

"…Authorities have not ruled out terrorism at this time. A frequented site for tourists, the ancient ruins of Teotihuacan in Mexico, came under attack only weeks ago by an unknown group. No one has claimed responsibility for these attacks, but it is suspected that there might be some connection to the attacks on other ancient sites in the recent months. These sites include the Coliseum in Rome and the Great Sphinx in Egypt. Authorities are baffled by these attacks. Motive has not been ascertained at this time, leaving investigators wondering if there will be another attack in the near future and, if so, to what end? Thankfully, the attacks of Teotihuacan took place at night when tourists and locals were not in the vicinity. Right now, we have our correspondent, Megan Crusher, on location to get some local reactions to the recent destruction. Megan."

The image on screen shifted to a woman with long dark hair, tied up into a bun. She looked jet-lagged and sweaty from the apparent humidity. In the background, ancient step pyramids stood with large chunks of the structure blown away.

"Thank you, Linda. We've been on site since the attacks took place over two weeks ago. Locals here are outraged that anyone would destroy a piece of their rich history. For many locals, the tourism business is a sole means of income and now that has been ripped away from them. Authorities here have been inundated with numerous reports on what might have happened, but no real leads have come to light. In lieu on any real explanation, many of the locals have taken to blaming the ancient Aztec feathered serpent god Quetzalcoatl, saying that they have angered the deity by not honoring their old traditions. Some locals have even gone on to say that the feathered serpent was spotted flying away from the ancient site. Scientists have no proof indicating such a creature exists, but unfortunately for the local population, this has only raised more questions. This is Megan Crusher, for Beacon News, back to you, Linda."

"Thank you, Megan. Please stay tuned as we continue our investigative coverage of what the public has come to call, 'The History Bombings'. I'm Linda Welz, for Beacon News."

Osiris turned off the holo-display. "Well, looks like we are terrorists now."

"They can call us whatever they want. As long as no Earthborn gets hurt, we are doing our job," Alana said, as she closed her eyes to meditate once again.

"Does it matter that we didn't blow up the pyramids? It was the Fallen, and that crazy dragon thingy," Wayland said, between mouthfuls of food.

"Technically, we did blow you up," Ronin said chuckling. "A fine piece of strategy, Osiris."

"Yeah, don't remind me," Wayland replied. "I'm still mad at you guys for that. But, still. Shouldn't it matter that people know who the actual bad guys are?"

"Nope. Doesn't matter in the slightest," Osiris said irritated. "Never mind we're trying to save their skins from the Fallen. Ungrateful, gits."

"The Earthborn must not know," Alana said quietly. "The Codex decrees that we protect them. Nothing more. After we are gone from this Earth, the histories will reflect our deeds and we will be revered."

"Doesn't do me any good when I'm dead, love."

"People aren't dumb. We should just tell them," Wayland countered.

"It's not that simple, Wayland," Alana said.

"First, we must smite our enemies," Ronin said vehemently. "Then, the bards will sing our praise. You'll see, Wayland, Smith's Son."

"As long as we don't die in the process, I'm in," Wayland said.

CHAPTER SEVEN

REUNION

Max and Charlotte ascended the stairs that led to the Great Hall of the palace. Every few steps, the stairway was adorned with golden banners with a dragon emblazoned on it.

"What does the dragon mean, Charlotte?"

"That is the symbol of my House… my family crest, if you will," Charlotte said, as she glanced at the banners dancing in the wind. "It is called the Infinity Dragon."

Max looked more closely at the dragon and realized that the body of the mythical creature twisted around to form the mathematical symbol for infinity. "What does it mean?"

"It embodies the idea that eternal paradise can only be achieved through infinite faith. The Dragon represents wisdom and peace. These two characteristics make infinite faith possible. This is how Lemurians try to live their lives - Eternity through faith."

"Plus, dragons are pretty cool," Max said absentmindedly.

Charlotte laughed, the sound echoing off the marble walls of the palace. "Yes, I suppose you're right. It is *cool.*"

They reached the Great Hall. A red carpet ran the length of the hall starting at the entrance and ending at the raised dais where Queen

Alastriona sat. Max and Charlotte quickly walked to her and both bowed when they reached the throne.

"Welcome," she said warmly. "Thank you for coming so quickly."

"You didn't give us much of a choice, Mother," Charlotte said smiling.

"Yes, well... There are perks to being queen. Come. Let us move to my sitting room. We have much to discuss."

Alastriona stood and walked briskly to her right where a guard stood. As the group approached, the guard moved aside and the space on the wall where he once stood gave way to reveal a hidden door.

"Fancy," Max said to himself.

They walked through the door, which opened up to a large opulent room, full of large cushy chairs. The center of the room was dominated by an ancient circular wooden table, which was surrounded by large sturdy chairs. The table was decorated with several carvings that surrounded the Infinity Dragon that was carved in the center. Each piece of furniture and artwork in the room was of the finest quality, but Max only had eyes for the people sitting at the table. There, only a few feet away from him were Plato and, more importantly, his parents. Max's eyes welled up from the torrent of emotions rolling through his mind.

"Mom," he croaked. "Dad?"

Lara stood, tears streaming down her face. "Maxy," she cried.

Max ran to her and wrapped his arms around his mother. He noticed immediately that his mother was thinner and seemed slightly fragile. His emotions burst from him as he cried. "I thought you were, you were…"

"We're ok, Son," Jack said, as he stood and hugged both Max and Lara simultaneously. "We're ok."

All of Max's insecurities about whether his parents were still alive or not washed away like sand in a passing tide. He felt as if he could breath easier and the unexplainable weight that seemed to press down on him at every waking moment of his existence, since he lost his parents at St. Margaret's church, evaporated.

"But, how?" Max croaked. "Where…"

"They were captives, Max," Plato said a few feet away. "They were being held by the Fallen in a secret base in Antarctica."

Max slightly pulled away from his parents to look at Plato. His mentor looked travel worn and exhausted. "Master, thank you. Thank you for finding them."

"I told you I would not rest until we found them," Plato said smiling. "It just took a little longer than I expected."

"But how did you finally find them?" Max asked, as he wiped the tears on his cheeks with the sleeve of his shirt.

"We have Queen Alastriona to thank for that," Plato said, as he gestured to Alastriona who had taken a seat at the table next to Charlotte. "Because of the Seeing Stone that she provided, I was able to scry the location of your mother and father. To be honest, I don't know if I would have been able to find them otherwise."

Max turned to Alastriona and bowed deeply. "Thank you, Your Majesty. I owe you and your people so much."

"Family is the most important thing," Alastriona said, waving off his thanks. "It was an honor and pleasure helping you. Just seeing the Hunter Clan reunited is reward enough for me. Come you three, sit. As Plato will attest, we have much to discuss."

Max sat close to his parents, opposite the queen and Charlotte, while Plato sat adjacent to them all. Max stared at his parents. He couldn't believe that they were there sitting next to him. He felt like if he took his eyes off of them that they might vanish. Plato's voice cut across his inner thoughts.

"I'm sure you have many questions, Max. I've only recently found your parents a couple of days ago. We had to travel quietly back here to the Collective, so I am sorry I could not contact you sooner. Your father and mother were being held in stasis pods, or hab-units, and kept under sedation. It is one of the reasons I had so much trouble locating them. I couldn't feel either of their minds. A very disconcerting thing for me, especially in Lara's case."

"Why especially my mom?"

"We will get to that, Max, I promise. At any rate, with the help of the Seeing Stone, I was able to find them and mount a rescue mission."

"Why didn't you tell me you found them? I could have helped, Master." A slight semblance of betrayal washed over Max as he questioned his mentor.

"You were en route back from the Bermuda Triangle at the time, and I had to move quickly. You must understand, Max. Time was of the utmost essence. Ever since your parents were taken, I have been searching for them vehemently. Part of the reason I did not accompany you on your quest for the Tablets was because I was pouring much of my time and abilities in finding your parents."

"I'm grateful, of course, but I still don't understand why you didn't tell me. I could have done something. It killed me not knowing if they were still alive or not."

Lara placed a hand on Max's arm. "Plato was acting in your best interest, Max. We are all together and safe. That's what matters."

"I know. You're right," Max conceded. But, he was still having trouble accepting the fact that he was left in the dark about his parents' situation. He felt that Plato had no right to keep that from him.

"You had your mission to complete, Max. No matter how much I wanted to have you with me when I rescued your parents, you had your responsibilities as the Key," Plato sighed. "Sometimes, our responsibilities supersede family obligations, unfortunately. Trust me, I did not want to send you, Alana, and the rest of your friends out into the world on a dangerous mission."

"Wait, you sent him where?" Lara asked, a hint of anger in her voice.

Max watched Plato squirm slightly. The action threw Max off a bit. He had never seen Plato act so uncomfortably before. Plato was always calm and confident. Now, he looked like he was preparing to be scolded.

"Lara, we had to make our move against the Fallen. Max was our only hope in finding the Leviathan."

"You sent Max to find the Leviathan?!"

"Now, Lara, remain calm. Max has been through a great many things. He has grown both in maturity and power since you last saw him."

"How can I be calm? You sent your only grandchild to fight against the Fallen? He's only 16!"

"Lara, you know I would not risk Max getting…"

"I'm sorry… what?" Max asked quickly.

The conversation came to an abrupt halt. Jack sat back with a smirk on his face. Lara placed her hands in her lap, her lips pursed, staring intently at Plato. Both Alastriona and Charlotte sat quietly, their faces devoid of any emotion.

Max cleared his throat. "I think I'm confused. Did you say grandchild, Mom?"

"Well…" Lara began.

"Your mother is my daughter," Plato said softly. "And you are my grandson."

Max's mouth opened, but words seemed to fail him.

"We were meeting Plato in London, Max," Jack said. "We were going to introduce you, and tell you about…" Jack waved his hand around, "… all of this."

"Why didn't… why didn't you…"

"Why didn't I say anything?" Plato said. "Honestly, Max, we simply didn't have the time. After we first met, I left the Citadel to lead the search parties for your parents. My daughter was missing. I was going to find her. Directly after the events at the Sphinx, Vincini visited us and the mission to find the Tablets of Destiny was lain before you. Again, no time. That brings us to the present. I suppose there were moments when we could have talked about this, but the timing never felt right. I am sorry for keeping this from you."

Max nodded slowly.

"Imagine. I have been looking for the next Key of the Atlantean people for most of my adult life, all 11,000 years of it. Give or take. Then, my own grandson is born and all the signs pointed to you being the next Key. That is why your parents and I decided that it was best to spirit you away from the Citadel when you were born, away from the Atlantean world, to be raised as an Earthborn. We were hiding you in plain sight. If the Fallen knew about you, they would have hunted you and most likely killed you. So we kept it all a secret. The fact that you or your mother had any connection to me was buried away and kept secret to everyone but your father, of course."

Max still nodded his head slowly.

"Maxy, are you alright?"

"Uh... yeah, I guess. It's uh... it's a lot to take in. I mean, you'd think I'd be used to hearing unbelievable things by now, but you know..." Max laughed nervously.

"Max, we have to talk more about this in length. I'm sure you have many stories to tell us and we have a lot to fill you in on, but I think we have bigger issues we have to talk about right now," Jack said, looking back at Plato. "Plato, what news do you have about the Fallen's troop movements?"

"Yes, of course," Plato said. "We will discuss family matters soon enough. Her Majesty must hear of the intel our agents have acquired."

Max let out a small sigh, grateful for the change of subject. Oddly enough, he found comfort in focusing his attention on fighting the Fallen. It was his new normal.

"It is as we have feared," Plato continued. "The Fallen are amassing their forces with the intent of marching on the Collective. According to our spies, they now view the Collective as a threat."

Alastriona's shoulders sagged slightly and she rubbed her eyes. "I knew this was coming, of course. The moment I gave Max and his friends access to the Great Library and knowledge of the Tablets of Destiny, I knew this day was in our immediate future."

Max instantly felt guilty.

"I knew what I was getting into Max," Alastriona said, reading Max's emotions. "It was a decision that I would repeat if presented the choice again. Take heart, young Key."

"Well, maybe we can move the Tablet that we have, away from the Collective. Lure the Fallen away from your people. We can even spread rumors that I have left the Collective, and that we are no longer allies," Max said hopefully.

Alastriona smiled wearily. "I appreciate your sentiment, Max, but the die has been cast. As I've said, I knew what I was doing when I decided to help you. Maybe the Collective should have gotten involved centuries ago, but whatever the case, the Fallen have pushed too far this time. They forced my hand the moment they decided to use the Leviathan in their efforts against the Order of Light. That weapon will destroy all life on this planet. The decision of not destroying that accursed machine long ago has finally come back to haunt me."

Charlotte took her mother's hand and held it tightly.

"So, what is the next move?" Lara asked Plato.

"We have to help the Collective, of course. I will recall all of our agents and bring what security details we have at the Citadel to help defend this mountain. Unfortunately, if our intel is correct, that will not be enough."

"So we take the fight to them," Jack said. "Strike before they can completely assemble."

"We do not have any information on the whereabouts of this force," Plato answered. "We only know that a force of considerable size is coming."

"How is this going to go unnoticed by the Earthborn?" Charlotte asked. "The Fallen would expose themselves. The Earthborn Americans will not take an armed force on their soil lightly, not in this day and age."

"An excellent question," Plato said. "I can only guess on how Malus and his forces are going to overcome this obstacle. I do not think he would risk going to war with the Earthborn just yet, unless, of course, he had full control of the Leviathan, which he does not. Our saving grace in all of this is that we have one of the Tablets of Destiny. Without both Tablets, Malus cannot activate the Leviathan."

"It's all moot if we don't figure out a way to defend the Collective. If we lose here, the Fallen will gain control of the Leviathan," Lara said.

Max sat quietly and listened. He now knew that his parents have been part of this world of Atlanteans far before he was even born, but he was still having trouble reconciling the fact that his parents were freely talking about how to defeat the Fallen. Only months ago, they were in their house, discussing a family vacation to Egypt.

"Can we not just destroy the blasted thing?" Charlotte asked. "If we destroy the Tablet then even if the Collective falls, the Leviathan remains a non-factor."

"That is another problem we have. The Tablet is imbued with the power of the Great Crystal," Plato said. "No one, not even Venator himself, truly understood the full potential of the energy from the Crystal. Now that the Tablets are active, we do not know how to destroy them. Destroying the Leviathan is an option, but the Tablets are not."

"Well, Max gave the Tablets their power. Couldn't he take the power away?" Charlotte asked.

"You did what now, Maxy?"

"It's a really long story, Mom."

"Later, Lara," Plato said.

Lara frowned. Max knew that look all too well. He was going to have to face his mom soon enough.

"It wouldn't work without the other Tablet," Jack said, as he adjusted his glasses. "I've studied the Tablets' lore in depth. Each Tablet is symbiotic of the other. If you try siphoning the power from one and not the other, you could potentially cause an overload, which might lead to unforeseen effects on the Leviathan itself. Who knows what type of failsafe measures DaVinci and Wayland the Smith incorporated into the Leviathan. If the machine were to go into a self-destruct mode, the aftermath could be catastrophic on the surrounding populace around the Bermuda Triangle, if that is where it still is. The Fallen might have moved it, although that would be a herculean task."

"Yes, but these are all educated guesses. I believe my daughter makes a valid point," Alastriona interjected. "If we find that we cannot hold the forces of the Fallen at bay, I believe that the Key should attempt to siphon the power from the Tablet in our possession. There is a chance it could render the Leviathan inoperable."

"Yes, Your Majesty, but the chance that the Leviathan initiates its self-destruct sequence, killing thousands in the immediate area, is equally possible," Jack said.

"I hate to sound callous, but thousands pale in comparison to the millions that will die if the Leviathan is activated and unleashed," Alastriona said.

"She's right, Jack," Lara said, as she sat back in her chair. "We have to consider that Max might be the only chance we have of destroying at least one of the Tablets."

Jack nodded thoughtfully.

"Which brings us back to the question at hand. We will deal with the Tablet when the time comes, what we have to do now is figure out how to defend the Collective," Plato said, rubbing his eyes.

"We only have a small security detail and the Vanguard," Alastriona said. "That gives us roughly two hundred possible soldiers."

"With our field agents and Citadel security, we have a little over five hundred troops to command," Plato said. "I'm afraid seven hundred troops will not be enough. Our intel reports the Fallen numbers are in the thousands."

"Can we reach out to the other Houses, Plato? Maybe even the Guilds?" Alastriona asked.

"I do not know. There has not been a Gathering in hundreds of years. I'm not certain where some of the Houses' loyalties lie."

"I know of a few House Masters that have no love for the Fallen," Alastriona said. "We can at least reach out to them."

"As do I. Hopefully, between the two of us, we will have a quorum. If we can gather enough of their numbers to our side, maybe the Fallen will call off the attack altogether. Save us from any unnecessary blood shed."

Plato looked over to Max. "What say you, Max?"

"Me?" Max answered nonplussed. "I don't know how to defend a city, Plato."

Am I supposed to call him Grandpa now? Weird.

Plato smiled slightly. "It's customary for the Key to have a say in meetings that affect the whole of the Atlantean people. That is your role now, for better or worse."

Max nodded tentatively. "Well, sounds like we are about to get into a fight with a bigger, badder, group of people. Makes sense to reach out to friends for help. Except, we'll essentially be asking them to risk their lives for us, maybe even give their lives for us. I don't know if I'm ok with that."

"If the Fallen win, if the Leviathan is used, many more could potentially perish," Charlotte said quietly.

Max frowned. "Yeah, I guess you're right. What choice do we have then? We have to ask for help."

REUNION

"It is settled," Alastriona said, nodding her head solemnly. "The Council of Ancients will have a Gathering."

CHAPTER EIGHT

VICTORY OR DEATH

Crystalized breath billowed out from underneath Simon's parka hood in the frigid arctic air. His face was shadowed from outside view, giving him a foreboding look. He stood quietly next to Primus as they watched over the proceedings in front of their secret base. At least, it had been a secret, until the facility was breached only a few days prior. Primus nodded ominously at a woman standing in front of a group of soldiers who were all on their knees in a line. She was the new commander Primus assigned to the base. Its prior commander was now on his knees in the snow. The soldiers were not afforded simple comforts as the warm parka Simon was wearing. They had been stripped of their armor, weapons, and most of their clothing. Shivering in the sub-zero weather, they awaited the inevitable.

The newly appointed base commander stood in front of the men, carrying a long metallic spear. She pressed a button on the spear's shaft and the jagged blade on the business end of the weapon blazed and came to life. A red-hot glow radiated from the blade, as snow sizzled against the immense heat it generated. The phrase, *'a hot knife through butter,'* came to Simon's mind.

Primus stepped forward. "This is an unfortunate juncture. To lose an entire battle group in one fell swoop is disheartening." Primus swept his hand in the direction of the kneeling soldiers. "The seven of you have failed your mission, failed Lord Malus, and most of all, failed your brothers and sisters of The Enlightened. Now, you must pay the ultimate price." Primus turned to face the crowd of soldiers that encircled the kneeling men. "The enemy came into our base, *our house*, and took the renegades, Jack and Lara Hunter. The betrayers strolled into our fortified facility and were met with little to no opposition." He twirled and pointed accusatorily at the kneeling soldiers once again. "On their watch." Primus made a fist and raised it slightly. As he did, the seven men rose into the air, their feet barely scrapping the ground. "Know this - The Enlightened cannot carry out their righteous mission, when there are those of us who are not fully committed to the cause. Because I am feeling generous, these seven individuals will be afforded a warriors death, by the blade." Primus glanced at Simon. Their eyes locked. "This is how failure is dealt with in THIS order. This is the ONLY path. Victory or death!" his voiced bellowed.

The gathered soldiers echoed his sentiment. "VICTORY OR DEATH!"

The new commander stood abreast with the seven soldiers who stood just a few meters away. She raised the blazing spear, and launched it with practiced ease. The missile of black metal and fire flew through the air at an alarming speed and ripped through the torsos of the flailing victims. The violent kicking of the soldiers quickly ceased, and from their boots dripped deep red blood onto the pristine snow beneath them.

68

The commander pressed a button on her gauntlet and the spear circled back, propelled by an unseen mechanism within its shaft, and flew into her waiting hand.

Primus released his telekinetic grip and the soldiers fell like ragdolls. "Get this cleaned up, Commander. Prep for breakdown and evac. This facility is compromised."

"Yes, Praetor, right away," she said, as she flourished her spear and bowed.

"I hope that you will fare better than your predecessor, Commander. It would be a shame to lose you, especially right after your promotion."

The woman nodded and strode away briskly, already barking orders.

Simon watched as Primus walked back to where he was standing. He noticed that Primus's shoulders sagged slightly, and the man had a haunted look about him.

Primus stood next to him staring out into the vastness of the frozen tundra. "Necessary evils," he sighed.

Simon glanced up at him. "Yes, Praetor. Failure is not tolerated." Simon looked out onto the landscape. "But…"

"But?"

"It, uh, seems to be a waste of manpower."

"Perhaps, Simon. Perhaps. It is always a waste to lose our own kind. We Atlanteans are family, but even family needs to be culled from time to time."

Primus's words seemed almost questioning.

Simon shifted his feet. "I suppose, Praetor. Funny you should mention family, actually. Did I tell you that I saw Osiris on my last mission to procure the Tablets," he prodded.

"I read your After-Action Report. I am aware."

"He looked well," Simon said, with forced insouciance. "Well, at least he did before he dove into the ocean as their ship exploded."

Primus laughed faintly. "According to your report, that was right after he threw a knife into you, correct? You know, I taught him to throw knives when he was a boy. I see my training stuck," he said, as he glanced at Simon's leg.

Simon absentmindedly rubbed the area where the knife was buried only weeks ago. His Atlantean physiology long since healed the wound, but Simon remembered his surprise with the skill in which Osiris wielded the knife, but mostly, he remembered the pain. "You sound pleased your son is still alive."

"Of course. He is my son. When you have lived millennia, one realizes that one undeniable truth remains constant; family is the most important thing we have in our lives. No matter what disagreements we might have with them, in the end, they are all that matter."

"The Order of Light see us as the enemy. The Fallen, they call us. We are horrible monsters to them. How will your son ever reconcile with what you have done?"

"Osiris will see the truth of things once this war is over. You will soon realize, young Simon, that perspective is a fickle thing. History books are written from certain viewpoints and what people remember is based on one thing alone."

"What might that be, Praetor?"

VICTORY OR DEATH

"Those who win the wars, write the history books."

Simon nodded slowly. The sun was low on the horizon, its beautiful light mingling with the atmosphere. But, for all its splendor, it could not penetrate the icy air that permeated everything. He watched his breath coalesce and vanish in the dimming light. "Sometimes, I wonder what my sister must think of me, now that she knows I am alive. How will she remember me when this is all over? Will she see me as a betrayer, or eventually as a hero?"

"When this war is done, we shall see. For now, shield your mind as we prepare for the invasion. I believe Elder Plato possesses a Seeing Stone. It would explain how he found this base, and liberated the Hunters. He may attempt to glean information from us to gain an advantage. Bury these thoughts of your sister. We do not want Plato alerted to what we are planning. You have been given a great task, Simon. You must focus on your training."

"Yes, Praetor. They are buried."

CHAPTER NINE

THE GATHERING

Several days passed and Max found himself in the same meeting room in the palace of Queen Alastriona. This time, all of his friends were with him. Alana sat by his side, protectively, straight backed and prepared for anything. Earlier in the day, Alana explained to Max that, in the past, Gatherings of the Council of Ancients sometimes attracted nefarious individuals with the intent of assassination. Houses, and even Guilds throughout history would fight and wage war with one another, so subversive tactics were utilized to destroy ones opposition. Max tried to assure Alana that any attempt of a would-be assassination would likely never come to fruition. However, Alana always adopted the philosophy that one is better off erring on the side of safety rather than falling victim to an evil ploy and being proverbially 'sorry' for not taking actions to mitigate any threats.

They all sat around the large wooden circular table that was in the center of the room. They waited, along with Plato, Lady Sotera, and Max's parents, for the delegation that was comprised of the Ancients.

Tell me again, Alana. Who are these people we are waiting for?

The Council of Ancients is an elected governing group of Atlanteans who convene in times of strife, Alana pushed. *Plato founded the first one, centuries ago during the Cryptid Wars, and it was from that Gathering that wrought the tenuous treaty between the Earthborn leaders and Atlanteans. The Council has not been called on since. As the years have passed, members of the Council have changed, but their purpose still remains.*

With his fingertips, Max traced along the ancient grain of the wood and noticed the Atlantean glyphs that adorned much of the surface of the wooden slab. To his surprise, he could read the glyphs. At least some of them. Knowledge, that he didn't know he possessed, sometimes came to the surface of his consciousness, which could be attributed to the Recall process, a telepathic procedure Alana performed on him some months back. Max was able to access information he learned in the past, but information such as this, reading ancient Atlantean glyphs, was something he could not explain. It wasn't something he had ever learned. It was as if the knowledge was implanted in his mind, but from where he did not know. The unease he felt of not knowing frightened him. His mind felt violated.

"This is the round table," Max said quietly, to no one in particular. "King Arthur's round table." He glanced at Osiris quickly, who was leaning back in his chair dozing off.

Alana leaned over to him and whispered, "That is correct, Max. Did the queen tell you its story?"

"No, it's written here." He thumbed a groove of a glyph carved into the table. "Arthur Pendragon once ruled Lemuria?"

"When did you learn to read the ancient language?"

"I don't..."

73

THE GATHERING

A cacophony of trumpets and drums sounded unexpectedly as a herald entered the room. Osiris, who was leaning back in his chair with his eyes closed, nearly fell out of his seat, startled from the sudden din.

"Bloody hell. Is the Queen of England here?" he spluttered.

Plato, Lady Sotera, Ronin, Jack, Lara, and Alana stood from their seats. Their eyes expectantly fixed on the entrance of the room. Max, Wayland, and Osiris looked around bewildered.

"Stand," Alana hurriedly whispered. Max complied quickly, acquiescing with Alana's expertise in formal Atlantean matters. Seeing that Max stood, Wayland followed suit. Osiris, on the other hand, remained seated, almost stubbornly. It was a position that he was completely content with and he would have gladly stayed in. Auggie derailed Osiris's plans of relaxation and generally insolent behavior as he calmly walked over from the wall he was standing by and gently lifted Osiris into a standing position.

"Come, Guardian Pendragon, we mustn't be rude," Auggie said matter-of-factly.

"Alright, alright, you git. Get off! I'm standing... you happy?"

Max did his best to hide his amusement, but he was failing terribly as his shoulders shook from barely subdued laughter. Alana gave him a swift elbow to the ribs, and Max's smile rapidly turned into a grimace.

The herald cleared his throat. "The esteemed Council of Ancients recognizes and welcomes High Chancellor Lor Mammon of the Merchant Guild to the Gathering."

A tall slender man entered the room. He wore a white robe that was accented with gold thread and filigree. He had an uninterested air about him as he moved gracefully across the threshold of the entrance. His gaze never once drifted to the others in the room. Instead, he seemed to focus his stare far ahead of himself. Max frowned at his haughty demeanor, and as he continued to regard the pompous individual he noticed the man's chest. Embroidered on his robe was a golden disc, which resembled a coin, and on that coin was a depiction of the Atlantean glyph that represented the Founder. It was highly stylized in its calligraphic state and barely resembled the, oft times, simple symbol Max was used to seeing. The image exuded opulence, which seemed perverted and out of place to Max. Lor Mammon found his seat at the expansive circular table and remained standing, gazing back at the entrance he'd just come from.

The herald spoke again. "The esteemed Council of Ancients recognizes and welcomes First Speaker Sermo Trajan of The Speakers Guild to the Gathering. Sermo Trajan walked into the room and bowed gracefully to the queen. He wore jet-black robes, which were in stark contrast to his long silver hair. Around his neck, a silver medallion hung. Its intricate markings coalesced to form, what looked like to Max, a clenched hand wreathed by a braid of rope. Trajan had refined features, and everything about his visage bespoke sophistication and poise. Max could even smell the man's cologne as it permeated through the room.

"I am honored to be in your presence once again, *Sarratum* Alastriona. It does my heart good to have this council together again, as it was in the days of old. We are further blessed by the ever-giving Founder to have the Savai in our presence. An honor to finally make your acquaintance, young Key."

Trajan turned and gave Max the same bow that he just proffered to the queen. Max bowed in return, not knowing if that was the proper decorum or not. As he stood straight, he looked at Alana from the corner of his eye who nodded her approval almost imperceptibly. Max felt relief wash over him.

"Yes, First Speaker, it is good to see you too," Alastriona said lazily, as if she was too tired to deal with the all too familiar eloquence of Trajan.

Trajan smiled brightly and walked over to his seat.

The herald eyed at the entrance nervously. He glanced back at Queen Alastriona, who gave him a curt nod to continue the proceedings. The herald swallowed and his gulp was audible as he looked back to the entrance. "The esteemed Council of Ancients recognizes and welcomes Lady Sif Sekhmet, Clan Chief of the House Ariston, representing the Warrior Guild, to the Gathering. Lady Sif stormed through the entrance, obviously perturbed. She pulled a menacing knife from a scabbard on her hip and pointed it at the herald.

"Az Anu, Ni daku tu!" she bellowed.

By the Founder, I will kill you. Max's mind instantly translated the ancient Atlantean language.

How did you know that? Alana pushed, as she read his thoughts.

Max shrugged, as he continued to watch the proceedings. He didn't want to let Alana know how much he was shaken by the sudden influx of knowledge.

"Please, Lady Sif," Alastriona said calmly. "I'm rather fond of my herald."

"The Ariston Clan does not have time for pomp and circumstance, Your Majesty. I told this fool that I did not want an introduction. I am a warrior. What use does a warrior have for ceremony?" Sif said through gritted teeth, her knife still trained on the trembling herald.

"For me, my lady," Alastriona said gently. "You know I'm old fashioned. My herald was merely carrying out my wishes."

Sif sheathed the knife with practiced grace, and nodded curtly. The herald gratefully bowed, clearly relieved that he would not be turned into a pincushion. "Az tu, Sarratum."

For you, Your Majesty.

Sif walked over to Lady Sotera and they embraced.

"Good to see you, Sif. See you haven't lost your sparkling personality," Sotera laughed.

"You're one to talk," Sif said, her voice still stern, but with a touch of amusement.

The herald continued cautiously. "The esteemed Council of Ancients recognizes from the room, Lady Sotera, Clan Chief of the House Ferrum, representing the Craft Guild, to the Gathering."

Sotera bowed slightly toward Queen Alastriona and nodded her greeting to the rest of the people at the table.

"The Council also recognizes from the room Elder Plato, Master of the Cleric Guild and Leader of the Order of Light."

Plato performed the ritualistic bow and acknowledgements. His performance seemed more natural and warm compared to Sotera's. The Clan Chief of the House Ferrum looked bored and anxious to leave.

THE GATHERING

"The Council of Ancients also recognizes the esteemed guests in attendance. Who sponsors these individuals?"

"I, Plato of the Cleric Guild, sponsor all assembled guests to this Gathering."

"So shall it be written," the herald responded. "The Gathering welcomes the Ascended Key of the Atlantean people, the Founder's Speaker, bringer of balance, Maximus Lee Hunter.

Max winced at the mention of his full name. Only his mom ever used his full name, and it was usually only when we was in trouble.

"The Lady of the Light, High Lemurian, and ruler of the sacred realm, Queen Alastriona, chairs this Gathering. The Gathering of the Council of Ancients will now commence."

The herald bowed deeply then quickly left the chamber. The assembled group took their seats, the formal introductions completed. The large wooden doors thudded as they closed. Max felt like he was being locked in a vault. He didn't like enclosed spaces. Ever since when he was little and was stuck in the middle of a tube slide, mashed in between several other children, he had low tolerance for places that he felt he couldn't easily get out of. Beads of sweat began to form on his head and his breathing became rapid. Alana, instantly sensing Max's anxiety, slid her hand over on the table so their pinkies were slightly touching. Alana knew that an outright public display of affection would disrupt the proceedings, but the discreet contact between her and Max was enough for Max to regain his composure. The silence in the room lingered uncomfortably.

"Thank the Founder all that nonsense is over with," Sif said, breaking the obdurate silence.

"Aye," Sotera agreed.

Alastriona grinned. "Yes, I thank you all for enduring the traditions of this Council. After all, what are we without our traditions?"

"Here, here, Majesty," Trajan said.

Sif rolled her eyes. "I haven't the stomach for your sycophancy today, Trajan."

"My lady, I assure you…" Trajan started.

"Please…" Alastriona cut in. "I've called you all here to the Gathering under the most urgent circumstances."

"Yes, as you have said, Sarratum," Lor Mammon responded unemotionally. "How can the Merchant Guild assist the Sacred Realm?"

Alastriona took a moment, formulating her words. "As you all know, in all the dealings the Atlantean Empire has had through the millennia, the Collective of Lemuria has stood as a neutral party, a sanctuary for the war weary."

Sif quickly scoffed.

Max could almost feel the indignant aura Ronin was radiating behind him. You did not insult the royal family in his presence.

Alastriona pressed on, choosing to ignore Sif's blatant disrespect. "I know some of you on this Council do not agree with the Collective's way of life, but at every turn, the Collective has helped all of your Guilds and Houses in your time of need."

"I will concede to that, Your Highness," Sif said. "But, what of it? What is so important that you could not send us an email? You know our Guild is commencing with the Trials soon. This is an important time for our Houses."

Alastriona fixed her unwavering stare upon Sif. "It is time for Lemuria to collect, Lady Sif."

Sif stared daggers at Alastriona. The silence was palpable.

Plato cleared his throat, diffusing the rising tension in the room.

"Lady Sif, please. I implored her Majesty to call this Gathering. You see, The Fallen are on the move. They mean to attack the Collective."

"Forgive me, Elder Plato," Trajan said as he folded his arms. "The Order and The Fallen have been at odds for a very, very long time. The rest of us have been forced to step away from our people, our culture, to stay away from your feud. Why would we possibly want to get caught in the middle of the war now?"

Plato nodded several times, staring at the symbol of the Infinity Dragon. "Speaker Trajan," Plato's voice was calm and quiet. "The feud you are referring to has kept agents of destruction and chaos at bay for thousands of years. You have had the luxury of stepping away from your people while my Order has sacrificed and died to give you that luxury. I have been fighting this war before many of you *Ancients* were born. So, believe me, Speaker Trajan, when I say that the Fallen are coming and with them the means to destroy all in their path. The Collective is their first stop. After, they will come to either assimilate or destroy the rest of the Guilds in the Atlantean Empire." Plato's demeanor was altogether frightening to witness.

Trajan paled at Plato's assertion. "Yes... well. Master..."

"You are correct, Plato," Lor Mammon said plainly. "Every Guild in our paper Empire is symbiotic of the other. It is a tenuous equilibrium, one that even The Fallen has a part to play in. Checks and balances."

"Yes, but to openly oppose The Fallen..." Trajan began.

"Would you stand idly by while your supposed anonymity is stripped away?" Sotera asked angrily.

"Sif, would you please weigh in?" Trajan pleaded.

Sif's fingers were steepled, her judgmental gaze fixed upon Trajan. "The Warrior Guild will fight. As we always do. Our Houses fill your Order, Elder Plato. Make up your security details, Sarratum. They guard your precious vaults, Chancellor Mammon." Sif's eyes shifted to the different members of the Council as if sizing up a target. "We fight. That is what we do. If The Fallen want to fight, let them come. We haven't time for this politics, nor do we have any particular stake in the Collective's safety. The Fallen know where the Warrior Guild stands. If Malus himself wishes to take us down, I say it will be the last mistake that he makes."

"Strength and honor," Sotera said quietly.

"Strength and honor," Sif echoed questioningly. It was the traditional greeting the Warrior Guild utilized when addressing one another. It was also the Warrior Guild maxim.

Sotera looked at Sif intently. "Where is the honor in watching innocence die by evil hands, old friend?"

Sif's expression softened and she stood. "I am interim Battlemaster of the Guild, Sotera. I have to attend to the Trials. Once a victor is chosen, then the permanent Battlemaster will make a decision on your plight. I'm sorry... that is all I can do." Sif strode out of the meeting hall without a second glance. The door thudded ominously as it closed, giving the proceedings an eerie finality.

Ronin stood to go after Lady Sif, but Alastriona raised a hand. "Leave her be, Ronin. Sif is under a great deal of pressure. She's right, she does not owe any allegiance to the Collective."

"Be that as it may, the Warrior Guild and its houses would have been a welcomed addition to our ranks," Plato said, as he rubbed his face.

"The Merchant Guild will help finance any resistance the Collective and Order mount to supplant the oncoming advance of The Fallen," Lor Mammon said evenly. "A contract will be drawn assuring the Merchant Guild receives adequate protection as recompense for any monies passed in this endeavor. Do you agree, Your Majesty?"

Alastriona was used to dealing with Lor Mammon's pragmatic approach to every situation. It was a refreshing, albeit a cold and calculated, way of dealing with one another. "Agreed, High Chancellor."

Mammon stood gracefully and bowed towards the queen. "Very well, Sarratum. The contract will be delivered to you at first light, and I will assign a team of logisticians and accountants to help you prepare for the coming encounter with The Fallen. As always, it is a pleasure doing business with her Majesty." Mammon walked away the same way he walked in to the meeting. Eyes forward, straight-backed. Efficient.

"Well," Trajan said thoughtfully. "Mammon is nothing, if not predictable." He stood and faced the queen. "Most esteemed and pious ruler of the sacred realm, I must take my leave. The House of Speakers is with you. I will employ our network of *Sicarius* to gain as much information as possible on the dealings of The Fallen. I will ensure they report directly to your war ministers. Of course, intel is only as good as the generals who use it, but I digress."

"Take your leave," Alastriona said trying to hide her annoyance. "We will do our utmost to utilize your *Sicarius* intel properly. Your allegiance to this Council and this endeavor is most… welcomed."

Trajan bowed deeply. "You honor me, Sarratum. Until we are together again, I bid you adieu." Trajan turned quickly, his robes flourishing around him as he sauntered out of the room.

After the door closed behind him, the group looked to Plato. He was smiling and nodding to himself.

"What is it, Plato?" Alastriona asked nonplused.

"Trajan is right."

"Have you finally snapped, Plato?" Sotera guffawed. "Since when is Trajan right about something?"

"We need soldiers and a general to lead them," Plato said, still nodding and staring off into the distance. His head snapped to Alastriona. "I know how we can get both."

CHAPTER TEN

ROAD TRIP

The group shifted seats so they were closer to listen to Plato's plan. Auggie stood directly behind Plato; his chest projector was now emitting a geographical map of Mt. Rainer, the mountain home of the Collective of Lemuria. The map hovered over the center of the table. Its blue glow cast a ghostly light on everyone's face.

"It occurred to me right after Trajan left that our little meeting provided all the answers we need to accomplish our goals," Plato said excitedly. "My plan is two-fold. First, in order to defend this mountain, we will need a military strategist. Someone who will be able to use the intel the Sicarius gather in the most advantageous way possible."

Sicarius? Max pushed to Alana.

Political spies and assassins.

Whoa. I thought the House of Speakers was a bunch of stuffy politicians.

You would be surprised what they are capable of, Max.

"We all have skill in battle and most here have fought in one war or another, but to properly defend this area we need someone skilled in military operations," Plato continued.

"It's because my dad is leading The Fallen army, isn't it?" Ronin said with some disdain.

Plato's gaze fell slightly. "We are not sure who is leading the enemy force, Ronin…"

"It's alright, Master," Ronin said. "I know it's him. We need someone who will be able to counter my father's military strategy. He's the best military mind in the Atlantean Empire. That's why none of us are fit to lead our forces. Right?"

"We must plan for the worst-case scenario, yes, Ronin," Plato conceded. "As good as your father is, there is another Atlantean who could successfully concoct a plan to defend the mountain." Plato punched in a command on a tablet in front of him. "Auggie, if you please."

Information from the tablet was transmitted instantly to Auggie's positronic brain and his projection shifted. The mountain faded away only to be replaced by an image of a wizened old man.

"Dad, are you sure about this?" Lara said staring at the image.

"Lara is right," Alastriona agreed. "He has forsaken the Empire to pursue his own personal mission. You'll never get him away from Iga."

"Who…" Max started.

"Master Sun Tzu," Alana said contemplatively.

"The old Chinese dude that wrote that war book?" Wayland asked.

"The Art of War," Ronin said reverently. "A masterpiece of military strategy and tactics."

"Tzu is even crazier than you, Plato," Sotera said, shaking her head. "He's a hermit. Primus was his last student, and that was thousands of years ago."

"Is everyone in Atlantis crazy old?" Wayland asked in disbelief.

"The Ancients make up only 7.77% of the Atlantean race, best friend Wayland. So, no, not everyone is old."

"Man, you are on it, Auggie."

They exchanged a high five.

"Yes, Master Tzu is one of the Ancients. We have had favorable dealings in the past. I'm sure he will listen to reason," Plato said. "He just needs to be properly convinced."

"I'll go, Master," Max said. "I'm the Key, right? Maybe I can convince him."

"Max is right," Jack said adjusting his glasses. "Master Tzu would listen to the Key. Lara and I will go with him."

"Actually, I may need your help with the lockdown of the Citadel," Sotera said. "The two of you helped design many of the security parameters, it would be faster with you and Lara."

"Yes, and the three of you could work with our engineers to upgrade our systems here in Lemuria," Alastriona said.

"I don't want to leave Max," Lara said vehemently. "I will not separate my family."

"Elder Lara, I can go with Max," Alana offered.

"Alana is certainly capable and she has successfully protected Max on two separate missions now," Plato said thoughtfully.

"You sent him on two missions?" Lara asked exasperated.

"Well, technically, the first mission Max took upon himself," Plato said pleadingly.

"It doesn't matter!"

"Lara," Jack said softly. "Max is the Key. We knew the day would come when his safety would be out of our hands."

"No," she said flatly. "I'm his mother, Key or not. His safety will always be my responsibility."

"Elder Lara," Charlotte spoke up. "I, too, can accompany Max and Alana. I know Master Tzu and the Iga region. We will travel covertly and with haste. The three of us have made an excellent team in the past. I ask on behalf of my people. I know your expertise will help protect the people of Lemuria. The Hunters are legendary. With you here, overseeing our fortification, my people will have some semblance of hope."

"Well said, my daughter." Alastriona placed a hand reassuringly on her daughter's shoulder.

Lara looked up to the ceiling and took a deep breath. She glanced over at Jack who nodded slightly. Lara looked intently at Alana and the rest of Max's friends assembled at the table. "All of you have been there for Max when his father and I could not, and we will forever be grateful. I suppose that if he has to go on yet another mission, there isn't anyone else who I would want to be with him," she said begrudgingly. "You all would have made the Guardians of old very proud."

"Indeed," Plato agreed. "So, we all have our missions. I will utilize the Seeing Stone to scry for more Atlanteans willing to come to our side. Lara and Jack will assist Lady Sotera. Max, Alana, and Charlotte will go to Japan to speak with Sun." He frowned, lost in thought. "We haven't much time."

"What about the rest of us, Master?" Ronin asked. "Osiris, Auggie, Wayland Smith's son, and I can also accompany Max on this grand adventure."

"Actually, that brings me to the second part of my plan. The four Houses of the Warrior Guild will soon be engaged in the Trials of Kratos; a tournament used to decide whom the new Guild leader, what they call the Battlemaster, will be. With Primus out of play, the Guild needs to find a new leader quickly, before the Houses resort to in-fighting."

"The glorious Trials of Kratos," Ronin said excitedly. "I have dreamt of competing in that very tournament. To test one's prowess against the best of the best... Ah, it makes the heart pound like a war drum." Ronin's face suddenly looked crestfallen. "Outsiders are allowed only on special occasion. It's only happened once in the past thousand years."

"Yes," Plato said smiling. "But who better to request special invitations than the ruler of the Sacred Realm." Plato turned to Alastriona smiling.

"You wish to engage the Clan Chiefs directly," Alastriona stated, realization painted across her face. "The Four Horsemen. Get them on our side..."

"Correct," Plato said. "The four Clan Chiefs, commonly known as the Four Horsemen, command their respective ranks. Sif cannot request anything of the Guild, as interim Battlemaster, but if our own warriors garnered invitations and competed..." he said as he gestured to Osiris, Ronin, Wayland, and Auggie, "...if they could hold their own, maybe even win, we could gain favor in the Guild and possibly bring them to our cause. The Houses respect warriors, and acts of valor. What is more courageous than trying to defend the city of peace... Lemuria?"

Ronin stood quickly with his fist over his chest. "You honor us with such a mission, Master Plato. Our holy task will be completed. We will fight with righteous vigor and..."

"Whoa, whoa, whoa, people. Time out!" Wayland said in a panic. "Go fight in a tournament full of people who are part of the *Warrior Guild*? Their actual jobs are to be warriors?" Wayland's head was turning back and forth to everyone at the table. "You want me to be in this tournament... full of w-a-r-r-i-o-r-s?" He said the last word slowly with exaggerated articulation.

Ronin slapped him on the back. "Yes, friend Wayland, I know. The honor is almost too much to bear for a single person. Luckily, we are mighty. Never fear. We will be together."

"What? No! That's not..."

"Don't worry," Osiris said lazily. "You don't have to win. Just surviving the fight will be enough in the eyes of the Houses. If a few dozen bombs didn't kill you, what's one guy with a sword going to do to you?"

"They use swords?" Wayland's voice squeaked.

Plato nodded solemnly. "You know, I once said, nothing in the affairs of man is worth great anxiety. I was being ironic at the time. Yet, here we are, preparing for the fight of our lives, ultimately in service of man. The road ahead is rough. Make preparations. We have a war to win."

CHAPTER ELEVEN

7 NINJAS OF IGA

"So wait," Max said confusedly, as they walked to the awaiting drop ship at the far end of the Lemurian airfield. "We're going to Japan?"

Alana hefted a large bag on her shoulder. "Yes, that is correct.

"But, the dude's Chinese." Wayland said.

"Nationality and ethnicity do not always dictate one's place of residence," Auggie stated matter-of-factly.

"Too true, Aug. Too true, bro."

"Alpha Team, we are over there," Osiris said, as he walked towards a drop ship parked parallel to the one Max was going to.

"Since when are you guys Alpha Team?" Max scoffed.

"Since I'm on Alpha," Osiris said, turning around to face Max.

"Well... be careful, Alpha Team," Max said mockingly. "Get everyone home safe, Oz," he said more seriously.

"You worry too much, mate. I thought that was Alana's job."

Alana raised an eyebrow. "Someone has to take care of you children."

"It saddens me to be separated from you all," Ronin said. He took Charlotte's hand and bent to kiss it. "Especially from you, my love."

"Oh, here we go," Osiris said, as he turned and threw up his hands in frustration.

"I shall pray to the Founder that your mission is successful and I will beseech that he…"

"Her," Osiris said under his breath.

"…give you the strength needed to smite any that oppose your victory," Ronin said, still bowing before Charlotte.

"The Founder's will, be done, my beloved. Bring our people honor and our life-force will be joined again, in this life or the next."

"For Founder's sake," Osiris mumbled. "Come on, you lot. We've got a tournament to win. Max, Alana, Charlotte… good hunting."

"And to you, Oz," Alana responded.

Wayland grabbed Max in a giant bear hug. "Gonna miss you brother."

"I'll see you in a few days. Way… can't breaaaath, can't…"

Wayland promptly put Max down. "Oh, sorry bro. Still getting used to this growth spurt."

Max coughed a few times, catching his breath. "Yeah. So much… so much for being normal, eh?

"Normal is boring," Wayland scoffed. "Who wants to be boring?

"Yeah. Right." Max said laughing. They performed their prolonged handshake and hugged one more time.

"Be safe, Way. Remember - Always be afraid. You're invincible when you're scared," Max chuckled.

"Yeah. That won't be too difficult. I really got the shaft on the superpower lotto thing, huh?" Wayland said a little sadly.

"I dunno. Being untouchable, superstrong, immune to fire, and a freaking giant aren't too bad in my book, Way."

"Well, when you put it like that... I am kind of a badass," Wayland smirked.

"The baddest of the asses," Auggie said from behind them. "Come, best-friend-Wayland, we must depart."

"Right you are, my android amigo. Alright, Max. Peace be the journey, brother."

"Peace be the journey, Way."

The two friends walked to their respective transports. Max settled in to the seat next to Alana. The walls and floor were transparent from inside the flying vessel. Max loved that feature.

Across from them, Charlotte held a small metal object. Her eyes were closed and she was muttering something in ancient Atlantean. All the while, she rubbed the metallic object with her thumb. Max looked at it closer and realized that is was the symbol of the Founder.

"She's praying," Max said to himself.

"Yes," Alana whispered. "We will definitely need more of the Founder's help before long."

The dropship shuddered to life and rose, almost lazily into the air. Max watched the ground drop away as they lifted off. It was his favorite part. "I'm so glad we aren't taking the grid. I hate traveling like that. Felt like throwing up every time we went through a portal."

"Mmm." Alana agreed quietly. "Safer to keep EEG shut down anyway. Don't want unwanted guests accessing it."

"Yeah. How long is this trip going to take?" Max asked, to no one in particular.

Almost on cue, the pilot's voice came over the intercom. "Y'all sit back and relax now. You're sitting in the latest model of the X1 Phantom. This baby will get us to the land of the rising sun in just over two hours. If y'all need anything, just holler. It's an honor to be riding with the Key and his crew."

Max blushed slightly and waved up to the cockpit where the pilot and co-pilot were sitting. They gave him a thumbs-up.

Max looked over at Alana who had her eyes closed, but she was smiling broadly. "What?" Max asked embarrassedly.

Alana shook her head without opening her eyes. Her smile grew even larger. "Nothing. It's just nice to be a part of your crew."

"Stop making fun of me," Max chuckled, as he rubbed the back of his neck.

"Get some rest, Key. We're going to need to be sharp. Iga is said to be a dangerous region."

"Of course it is," Max sighed as he closed his eyes. "Night, Alana."

"Night."

*　*　*

"Coming up to the drop zone," the pilot's voice cut across his consciousness.

Max willed his eyes open and saw Alana doing a systems check on her M.A.R.S. armor. Max yawned deeply. "Go time?" he asked.

"Go time," Charlotte confirmed, as she sheathed the two halves of her bow blade on her back.

Max activated his armor by pressing a series of buttons on his gauntlet. "H.U.D.," he said softly. A user interface appeared before his eyes. The armor's neural link was functioning properly. "Systems check." A blue box appeared before his eyes.

> *Are you sure. Yes/No*

"Yes."

> *Sleep Mode During Systems Check.*
> *0.1% Complete.*
> *Estimated Time Left 3 Min 49 Sec*

"H.U.D., off."

The holographic image of his armor's user interface disappeared and he proceeded to systematically check all of his weapons. Alana looked over at him and smirked.

"What?" Max asked, without looking up. "Did I forget something?"

"On the contrary," Alana said, returning her attention to her own gear. "You're doing splendidly. I'm pleased you paid attention in our lessons."

It was Max's turn to look at Alana and smile. "You're kind of easy to pay attention to."

The dropship touched down and the cabin shook slightly. "We'll stay put, 'til you say, Savai," the pilot called from the cockpit. "Area secure and clear. Rear bay door opening. Clear the ramp."

The back of the ship opened, the top and bottom halves splitting horizontally in the middle. The cold metal gave way to the warmth of the outside sky. Orange and purple danced across the landscape as the sun made its final descent in the last moments of dusk. The sweet aroma of cherry blossoms that filled the interior of the ship reminded Max of summers past with his parents. Max stared at the landscape for a moment, lost in the majestic beauty of Iga, Japan.

"It's like looking at a painting," Max murmured.

"It is stunning, isn't it," Charlotte agreed.

"I've often thought that if I could choose anywhere to live, it would be in Japan," Alana said.

Max could almost hear the longing in her voice. "One day."

"Mmm. One day," she responded wistfully.

"Come," Charlotte said. "I have the map and directions uploaded to my suit's matrix. I'll send it to the both of you in case we're separated."

Max powered up his suit and almost instantly a message flashed in the corner of his vision. Max stared at the icon and blinked twice. The message opened and the map Charlotte had sent downloaded to his system. Max initiated the overlay protocols and the map converted to augmented reality mode. Wherever Max looked, the directions were laid out in front of him in real time.

"Alright, let's move," Alana said. "We'll stay in stealth mode and maintain radio silence. Keep a tight formation. Last thing we want is to be separated on this mountain."

Max liked when she went into tactical mode. She was a natural.

"Alana, may I take lead?" Charlotte asked. "If Master Tzu spots us, maybe he'll see me and recognize me. This whole trip might go a lot easier."

"Of course, Your Majes… wait, sorry, I forgot; Charlie in the field."

Charlotte smiled broadly. "Yes, thank you, Alana."

The trio moved out. They followed the path laid out on their heads up display. Max did his best to walk as quietly as possible, but the forest terrain made it very difficult for him. Every few yards, he stepped on a twig or in a particularly loud clump of dead leaves.

"Sorry," he whispered remorsefully, after the hundredth time of stepping on a twig. The snap of the twig echoed off the trees all around them.

"Radio silence," Alana said in a hushed tone.

"I still don't get why we're sneaking around," Max said quickly.

"Master Tzu moved to these mountains to get away from the world. Especially Atlanteans," Charlotte said quietly. "He doesn't want visitors. He might have put countermeasures in place to dissuade unwanted guests."

"Would it kill him to get email?" Max asked, as he looked around the forest with a newfound caution.

"Radio silence," Alana repeated, this time a little more forcefully.

"For what?" a female voice called out ahead of them. "The boy moves like a drunken bear looking for food."

Laughter, from several different people, emanated from the forest around them.

Alana turned the stealth mode of her suit off and she materialized behind the girl who was speaking to them. Her sword was drawn and its blade only inches from the girl's throat.

The girl's head snapped to the left. "Oh-whaa?! You, on the other hand, are very good. I didn't even hear you pass me! Well played."

Max and Charlotte materialized out of thin air, their cloaks deactivated.

"You shouldn't sneak up on people. It's considered rude in most parts of the world," Alana said calmly.

"Well, its sort of what we do here," the girl responded. "Have you noticed the outfit?

The girl was dressed in camouflage from head to toe. She even sported a mask that covered all but her eyes. The material was crafted to mimic their woodland surroundings. Max had difficulty focusing on her because her body seemed to phase in and out with the landscape.

"Um, you said we?" Max asked.

"We were just waiting for all of you to reveal your positions. Your fancy Atlantean armor has great stealth tech, except when you're stumbling around like…"

"…Like a drunken bear, yeah, we got it," Max said annoyed.

"Kogeki!" the girl commanded.

From all around them the forest seemed to come to life. Figures emerged from trees, bushes, and even the forest floor. All were perfectly camouflaged and they all carried deadly bladed weapons.

Seven Targets, Alana pushed.

They had Max, Alana, and Charlotte completely surrounded.

7 NINJAS OF IGA

"We are the Ninjas of Iga," the girl said proudly.

CHAPTER TWELVE

COVER CHARGE

Osiris swiped his sword to the right, cutting down the vegetation that blocked their path. The jungle canopy shielded them from the sun's punishing rays, but sporadic beams pushed through the plush leaves from the trees, spotting the ground with golden disks of light. The humidity left the air moist and almost suffocating. The M.A.R.S. armor Osiris and Wayland wore came complete with environmental conditioning, but despite the advanced technology that the suit was comprised of, the boys' sweat came down in sheets. Osiris idly wondered if Ronin's Lemurian armor was struggling with the humid heat and if Auggie's circuits were in danger of shorting out. The four travelers walked in a straight line, forging a path through the dense jungle landscape.

"Why…" Wayland wheezed.

"Why what?" Osiris called over his shoulder.

"Why can't we ever visit some place with air conditioning?"

"What?" Ronin queried at the end of the line, behind Auggie.

"Why can't our missions bring us to a nice hotel with room service or something. It's always someplace… uncomfortable."

Osiris barked out a laugh. "Where's the fun in that?"

Wayland nodded philosophically. "Well, I guess I can now mark the Philippines off of my list of places I haven't been."

"Sungadan, Philippines is a sacred place," Ronin said cheerfully. "This place is where some of the finest warriors have trained. Sungadan literally means 'entrance'. You enter as a student and emerge a warrior. It is no wonder that the Warrior Guild holds the Trials here. Two of the Four Horsemen hail from this region. That should be some indication of this area's importance."

"That's such a morbid name. Four Horsemen. Makes me think of the end of the world," Wayland mused.

"Once again, your instinct serves you well, best-friend-Wayland. The Four Horsemen are the four Clan Chiefs that lead each House in the Warrior Guild. It is theorized that the biblical reference could have come from this very group. Throughout history, the four Clan Chiefs have acted as Generals in many of the great wars this planet has seen. Their prowess in combat is almost unparalleled and they are feared by most. To battle with them, it is said, to court death."

"Warm and fuzzies, Aug. Warm and fuzzies."

"I have trained and sparred with the Horsemen before," Ronin said proudly. "They truly are spectacular in battle. That is why the Trials of Kratos are so important. The Battlemaster that rules over the Houses has to be not only skilled in combat, but also be trusted and respected by the Horsemen. The tournament is ancient. It was once the arena where wars were decided. It has evolved over the years to become the selection tool for the position of Battlemaster."

"So, why doesn't one of the Horsemen become the Battlemaster?" Wayland asked, as he fanned himself with a large leaf he picked up from the ground.

"It's happened before, back in the day," Osiris said, still hacking away at vines. When a Clan Chief requests to become the Battlemaster, he must defeat the other Clan Chiefs in single combat. Typically, the Clan Chiefs choose to remain in their posts. Becoming Battlemaster means they would have to leave their respective Houses and be responsible for the entire Guild. A clan is like a family. Leaving family isn't something most people are willing to do."

"Yeah, I know the feeling," Wayland said, almost to himself. "So, what's a Kratos?" he asked, trying to change the subject quickly.

"Not a what," Ronin said. "Kratos was said to be the originator of the Warrior Guild. When the empire was still young, so many thousands of years ago, Kratos was the best warrior and one of the founding members of the Atlantean Empire. It is said that those first Atlanteans communed with the Founder directly, as easily as we speak to one another now. What a glorious time that would have been."

"You exhaust me sometimes, bro," Wayland said.

"I think this is it," Osiris said, as he cut through the final vines blocking their path.

The four of them walked into a clearing. The jungle surrounding the area created a tall boundary that kept the clearing from unwanted visitors. A huge monolithic butte dominated the clearing. The top of the butte disappeared high above the jungle canopy.

"Why didn't we just fly to this clearing?"

"Because, Wayland, in the invitation that the queen received from Lady Sif, the instructions said we weren't allowed to. Probably some security thing. It wasn't you that was chopping through all the vines, now was it? So, stop complaining," Osiris said annoyed.

"Sorry, Oz. Geez. Here let me fan you; I think the heat is making you a little testy," Wayland said, as he used the oversized leaf to fan Osiris.

Osiris grinned and shoved Wayland's leaf away from him. "Get off you…"

"Contact," Auggie said, as two menacing looking blades shot out from his forearms. A shield dropped in front of his metallic face and all that was visible were his eyes, which now glowed red.

"Whoa, Aug, is this your new combat mode or something?" Wayland asked amazed.

"Eyes front," Ronin said, his own sword out and at the ready.

The group stared at the base of the butte. Its red rock was jagged and rough.

"Where, Aug?" Osiris asked. He spun the twin gladii around in a circle at his side.

"12 o'clock."

"I don't see…"

Wayland stopped speaking when he saw a shift in the rock face of the butte. A pair of lights began to glow. The shockingly green lights seemed to float roughly fifteen feet in the air. They shifted to the left, then to the right. Rocking back and forth. Wayland tried to strain his eyes. As he looked, he noticed a piece of the rock face seemed to be shifting with the glowing lights. "Wait… what is that?"

As he spoke, other green lights winked on and the glow from the combined power of the lights illuminated the outline of a massive humanoid figure. The two original lights glowed brighter, as if they were powering up. "Those are eyes, guys. Those are eyes! It's a giant rock thing," Wayland piped.

Auggie phased into a large Viking, carrying a battleax and a metallic shield. "It's a Golem," he said in a thick accent. "A Golem is a bio-mechanical construct that can be purposed for various tasks, best-friend-Wayland."

The Golem's eyes flashed and green energy beams shot at the four boys. They dove aside, barely dodging the attack. The beams blasted into the soil, sending rock and dirt flying all around.

"I think his task is to kill us, Auggie. Run!" Wayland screamed.

Osiris rolled to the side, as a chunk of stone came down from the blast. As he rolled out, he threw a flat metallic disc at the Golem's leg. The sharpened edge of the disc dug deep into the rock and metal that made up the shin of the behemoth. Osiris pressed a button on his gauntlet and the disc exploded. The Golems right leg burst into debris, as sparks from the mechanics, hidden under the rock façade, rained out. The rock machine dropped to one knee. It fired its green lasers from its eyes again.

Wayland stared up in shock, as he watched the green beams heading directly for him. He stayed rooted to his spot, petrified into inaction. Viking Auggie threw himself in front of Wayland, his shield raised. The beams struck home, blasting the shield with a steady stream of concussive force. Auggie leaned into the force of the beams. His feet began to sink into the soil beneath him.

Wayland looked and saw Auggie struggling against the pressure of the beams. His anger flared at the sight of his friend being attacked. In a moment of insane rage, he ran out from behind Auggie and made a dash for the Golem's other leg that was still intact. He lowered his shoulder, just like he learned in football practice and collided with the leg, head on. He laid all his strength behind the blow. His powerful legs were pumping, propelling him through the target. Wayland crashed through the leg, stumbling out onto the other side. A gaping hole in the leg was now present. Wayland punched clean through the appendage without so much of a scratch on himself.

The Golem flailed, as its internal systems began to systematically crash from the sustained damage. Its head thrashed left and right, sending the concussive beams firing erratically around the clearing. Ronin ran around the Golem and leapt onto its back. Another jump brought him to its neck. Ronin raised his bastard sword high above his head with both hands and brought the laser sharp blade swiftly down, puncturing the hardened rock skull of the Golem, straight into the central processing unit of their mammoth adversary. The beams shut off instantly and the Golem fell back. Ronin jumped off at the last minute and rolled away.

"Help!" Wayland yelled.

Osiris, Ronin, and Auggie ran to where the sound of Wayland's voice was coming from. "Help!" his muffled voice came again.

"Where are you, friend Wayland?" Ronin said, scanning their surroundings.

Auggie walked over to the Golem's hand that was now lifeless on the ground. He bent over and hefted the hand up and away to reveal

Wayland on the ground curled up in a fetal position. "Help!" he yelled again.

Osiris and Ronin stood over him and began to laugh.

"You are in no immediate danger, best-friend-Wayland."

Wayland looked up from behind his arm, his eyes wild with panic. Red faced, he stood up quickly. An imprint of his body was left in the ground, the weight of the Golem's hand evident. "I'm good. I'm good," he said shakily. "Just got crushed by a giant rock monster's hand. No b-b-biggie."

Ronin wrapped him on the back. "You are a true berserker, Wayland Smith's son. We are well met," he laughed.

"Well done, warriors," a voice called from above them.

The four companions looked up and saw a silver disc descending from above them. It was only a few feet in diameter and the disc's surface was highly polished. Wayland noticed his own reflection in the circular object, as it got closer. As the disc lowered, they saw a young woman standing serenely on it. She had radiant silver hair and deep blue eyes. She was dressed simply enough, but the simple clothes did not bely her beauty.

"No one has ever destroyed the Gatekeeper, as thoroughly as the four of you have, in the history of the Trials. Your teamwork is impeccable. That will not serve you in the next step of your journey, unfortunately," she said.

"Um, excuse me, pretty lady. But, who are you?" Wayland asked, as he puffed out his chest. "I'm Wayland, by the way, Wayland Smith. How ya doing?"

The girl tilted her head slightly and smirked. "I am the guide. Nothing more. You have passed the first Trial of Kratos, with the defeat of the Gatekeeper. Your next trial awaits. Conquer it and you will have earned your invitation to the great tournament."

"Oh, we've started, have we?" Osiris asked with surprise. "So, tell me, love, what is the next trial?"

"You must ascend and take your place in the arena," the guide said, as she began to drift upwards.

"The arena is up there? How in the hell do we get up there?" Wayland asked.

"A warrior must earn the right to compete. The climb is your payment," the guide answered.

"Worst day ever," Wayland said under his breath.

CHAPTER THIRTEEN

MOTHER EARTH

Max jumped back, as a menacing blade bit into the ground where he was standing only moments ago. The woodland ninja yanked on the chain that was attached to the blade, then arced the trajectory of the business end of the weapon back at Max's head. He dodged to the left and brought the blade of Excalibur up. The lightning from the sword trailed in its wake as it whistled through the air. The sword cut clean through the chain and Max's assailant stumbled backwards at the sudden loss of his weapon. Max tapped into his powers and pushed out a hand. His telekinesis shot forward and assisted the ninja's backward trajectory, flinging him into the trunk of a nearby tree. Max felt that same odd surge of power. He had to intentionally hold back, so as to not completely obliterate his assailant.

Max looked over his shoulder and saw both Alana and Charlotte engaged with two attackers each. Max didn't have much time to enjoy the girls' fighting abilities as he was kicked from behind. The blow wasn't as powerful as he was used to, but it still hurt.

"Not bad for an Earthborn, eh?" the girl said.

Max realized that the girl who kicked him was the same girl that first confronted them only minutes ago. "You're an Earthborn? Just a regular human?"

"When you say it like that, it hurts…"

She flung a shuriken at Max with deadly accuracy. It was all Max could do to dodge the deadly missile.

"…my…"

Another shuriken, this time aimed at Max's abdomen. Max jumped up and spun, his body almost horizontal, avoiding the flying dagger.

"…feelings!"

She threw another. This time, Max used his sword and swatted the metal blade out of the air. The girl threw down a pellet in front of her and, upon impact, a bulbous cloud of smoke appeared. Max swung Excalibur through the smoke, but nothing was there. In the distance, Max heard the girl giggle.

"Crap," Max said under his breath.

Alana deftly dispatched her attackers and threw them into Charlotte's attackers and the mass of ninjas fell in a heap before them. Charlotte joined the two hilts of her swords together to form the energy bow known as Victory. She took aim, her hand steady and calm. Max inadvertently stepped back when he heard the hum of the weapon. He knew it's destructive capability all too well. He almost felt sorry for the ninjas.

Charlotte drew her hand back, mimicking the act of nocking an arrow, and the crackling energy of Victory coalesced around her fist.

"Enough," a voice rang. "Training is done for today."

The ninjas stood and faced in the direction of a small man, who was perched several feet up on a branch of a tree. Max hadn't realized the man was up there. The ninjas removed their masks and bowed.

"Hai, Sensei. Domo arigato."

"D☐ itashimashite," the man responded.

Max looked at the ninjas. To his astonishment, they looked younger than he was. Barely even teens. They gathered their weapons and jogged away into the forest.

Charlotte looked up, placed her right fist in her open left hand and bowed. She was breathing heavily from the fight. "Wanshang hao, Shifu."

Alana bowed in the same manner.

Max, forgetting himself, simply grinned and waved. The man wore a white tunic over black flowing pants. At his side were two katanas – the daito and shoto, traditional weapons of the ancient Samurai. He looked to be middle-aged.

Which probably means he's thousands of years old by Atlantean standards, Max thought.

"I have not spoken Mandarin in many moons," the man said in English. He jumped off the tree branch and landed on the ground as soft as if he were simply getting off a stool. "Princess Charlotte, my how you have grown. You were only up to my chin, the last time I visited you and your mother in your mountain kingdom."

"Yes, Master Tzu. I remember."

"And, you, my dear one. Plato speaks of you as a proud teacher would of a prized and gifted student," he said, as he turned to Alana.

Alana smiled. A little sadly, Max noticed. "You honor me, Master Tzu.

"You're Sun Tzu!" Max exclaimed, realization dawning on him.

"You catch on quickly," Tzu chuckled. "I knew your predecessor very well, my young Key. He was my mentor and one of my dearest friends. I can see that you have the same zeal and curiosity that he possessed. Important traits for a Key, I suppose."

"Um, sorry, Master Tzu," Max said, as he clumsily bowed.

Tzu laughed again. It was a genuine laugh, free of malice or ill intent. "Do not worry about niceties, at least not around me. Come, walk with me. Tell me of your story."

On their walk, Max regaled Tzu with all the adventures he had experienced since he learned of the Atlantean world. Alana and Charlotte added to the stories, whenever Max stumbled.

"You see, Master. That's why we've come to you," Max said. "Everything has lead up to this. The Fallen are going to attack Lemuria. If The Fallen gain control of the Leviathan, innocent people will die. Also... we think Battlemaster Primus is leading the attack and we only have one chance to defeat him. That chance is you."

As they walked, the thick forest gave way to a peaceful village nestled in a small dell. The seven ninjas that attacked them earlier were now moving about the village, gathering water, stoking cooking fires, and other general errands. Max looked around in wonder. There wasn't a sign of any 21st century trappings.

"Ah, Primus. He was *my* most gifted and beloved student," Tzu said, as he looked at Alana. His voice was sad and full of regret. "But, unlike you, he seems to have strayed from the path. Very much not like him. This is very troubling indeed."

"Will you help us, Shifu?" Charlotte pleaded. "My people need you. This is our most desperate hour."

"Do you see these seven young people here in our little village?" Tzu asked, as he looked out onto the small cropping of buildings and huts.

Max, Alana, and Charlotte looked as well, and nodded.

This group of Earthborn and Atlantean is destined to become Ninjas of Iga. For hundreds of years now, I have trained my ninjas with a single purpose in mind - Protect those who cannot protect themselves. Seven at a time, I have trained them. Seven at a time, they go into the world to act as sentinels against injustice. At first, it was to protect this region of Japan. My beloved wife was a native here and it was here that we built our lives together. After she was taken from me, I decided the Ninjas of Iga would expand and act as silent guardians to all people in the world. I began to train Earthborn, helping them protect the people they loved and cared about. Year after year, century after century, seven at a time. This is what I have done. Now, you come to me and ask me to do what I have already been doing. I have been engaged in the war for much longer than most. Engaged, while others debated and squabbled over the issues that have plagued our world. My ninjas have been a force of good, battling against the darkness of The Fallen. Of course, I will help you. It is just and right."

Tears welled up in Charlotte's eyes. She fell to her knees and bowed in front of Sun Tzu. "Shifu, thank you. Thank you We thought you wouldn't agree. We thought…"

"Rise, my student," Tzu said, as he offered his hand. "You are a Ninja of Iga. You are family. We take care of our family."

"Wait, you trained here?" Max asked surprised.

"For a time," Charlotte said, smirking at some distant memory while she wiped her eyes. "Master Tzu taught me to wield Victory, my bow."

"May I, Charlotte?" Tzu asked, gazing at the swords that combined to form Charlotte's bow. "It has been a very long time since I've gazed upon Vijaya Dhanush."

Charlotte unsheathed her swords and placed them lengthwise in her hands. She then held them up, bowed, and offered them to Sun Tzu. Tzu grabbed them by the hilts and clicked them together to form Victory, or Vijaya in the ancient Sanskrit language.

"A work of art," Tzu marveled. "Your family is truly blessed to have one of the seven blades of legend in your possession."

"Yes, we are, Master," Charlotte said quietly.

"That thing scares me," Max said. "Those energy bolts are no joke."

"You struck the Key with Vijaya's energy arrows?" Tzu asked Charlotte in a berating tone.

"It's a long story, Master... a misunderstanding really. I apologized, of course," Charlotte said, her cheeks turning a slight shade of pink.

"How did you recover, Max? Elemental power is no small thing."

"Not sure what that is, Master Tzu. I was knocked out, I think, but I got better after awhile," Max said shrugging.

"He took the blow directly to his chest," Alana said. "It was by no means a glancing blow."

"I am very sorry for that, Max," Charlotte said.

Tzu gave the swords back to Charlotte. "Thank you, my dear. Please, go into the village. My students will have dinner prepared by now. Charlotte, will you show Alana the way? I would like to speak with our Key a moment longer."

Both Charlotte and Alana bowed and walked towards the blazing bonfire in the middle of the village. Max could smell the sweet aroma of roasting meat. His stomach growled.

"I have a favor to ask of you, Max."

"Of course, Master. Anything."

"I have a daughter. Her name is Ayako. She lives in the city of Kyoto, not far from here. I would ask that you go to her and bring her to Lemuria."

"Sure, no problem, Master."

"Thank you, Max," Tzu sighed, visibly relieved. "Now that I am choosing to align with you and Plato, The Fallen will surely target my only daughter. She is my whole world and I would like to have her close to keep her safe. I must make preparations here, and take care of my students before I leave. If you can transport Ayako, that would save us time. I can meet all of you in Lemuria."

"Sounds like a plan. The ladies and I will go and pick her up."

Tzu nodded. He looked content. "I will call ahead and alert her. She is also an accomplished ki master. She will be able to aid you in your energy fluctuations."

"What... what do you mean?" Max asked on guard.

"Max…" Tzu began tentatively. "Surviving a bolt from Vijaya is an incredible feat, even for someone like you. From the moment I saw you, I could read your ki, the inner energy that emanates from all living beings. Your ki is in a state of flux and needs to be balanced. What do you remember of your Ascension?"

Max was taken aback. He hadn't thought of the Ascension for quite some time. He couldn't remember exactly what happened, but he knew he felt different, a fact he had not shared with anyone.

"Bits and pieces, Master. Not much to be honest."

"Hmm. And, what differences have you noticed about yourself?"

Max began to feel uncomfortable. "I, um, feel the same pretty much," Max lied.

"Venator and I were close friends, Max. I grew up with Plato. I know what it means to Ascend. You have changed, but you are afraid. I understand. Please. I want to help you understand."

Max felt a little more at ease. Tzu knew what he was going through. He had seen it before with Venator. Max realized that Aside from Plato, Tzu was probably the best person to help explain what was happening. "I do… feel different. It's been little things. Stuff I shouldn't know, but I do."

Tzu nodded, "Yes, that is to be expected. What else? Have you noticed the elemental energies surrounding you?"

"Um, I don't know what that means, Master. I've noticed that my abilities *are* stronger; sometimes I can't control them. I feel like I'm absorbing energy and I can't contain it. Like, I'm going to explode."

114

"Yes. Elemental energy. The Casters call it Elemental magic or earth energy. It is probably one of your strongest abilities."

"What ability?"

Tzu smiled. "To tap into the ki of everything around you, even the earth itself."

Max shook his head doggedly. "Plato said I get my powers from the Great Crystal."

"That is true, but the Crystal is merely a conduit. It is the reason the Crystal was placed here in the first place by the Founders, so the theory goes. The earth is an incredible source of power. You will come to understand this more in time. For now, you need to learn to channel and control this ability. Once we are in Lemuria, I will show you how to meditate properly. It will be your first step to understanding the great mystery that is your existence as the Key."

Max had felt the changes after the Ascension. Changes he didn't understand and was too afraid to address. Knowledge that didn't belong to him, heightened powers… They all seemed to be invasive somehow. Foreign. They didn't belong to him; at least he didn't feel like they did. Max nodded. "Thank you, Master. What's happening… to me, it's a little… well, it scares me."

"All will be revealed, Max. Plato and I will guide you. First, we must protect the innocent. We must fight, and we must win."

CHAPTER FOURTEEN

TRIALS OF KRATOS

Osiris searched for another handhold. His muscles were overtaxed from the climb, but they were nearing the top of the butte, so the suffering would soon be at an end. He looked down to see how his companions were doing.

"You all right, lads?" he yelled down.

Ronin, who was only a few feet below him, looked up and smiled. "Beautiful day for a climb."

"Uggghh. Kill me now," Wayland grunted, another few feet below Ronin.

Auggie was at the end of the climbing team. "You are doing splendidly best-friend-Wayland." Auggie was still in his Viking form, large and lumbering.

"Thanks…," Wayland huffed, "…Aug. And, thanks again for catching me earlier."

"My pleasure," Auggie said quietly, as he stretched out a finger to a passing butterfly.

"So, I was thinking," Osiris said, as he strained his arm to reach another crevice in the rock face. "We need to come up with some kind of plan before we get up there."

"An excellent idea," Ronin said. "Once we enter the arena, fighters are forbidden to interact with one another until the actual bouts take place."

"Are either of you skilled enough at telepathy to make clear pushes to another person?" Osiris asked.

"Only feelings and intentions, not clear thoughts or messages," Ronin answered.

"What?" Wayland asked.

"Yeah, me neither," Osiris said, ignoring Wayland's question. "Would have been nice to communicate to each other when we get separated."

"I have installed undetectable communication devices in each of your armor," Auggie said.

"You did what?" Osiris asked confused.

"When did you accomplish this, Auggie?" Ronin wondered.

"Everyone was asleep during the trip here. I do not require sleep," Auggie said matter-of-factly.

"Undetectable? Are you sure?"

"97.7% projected success quotient," Auggie said. "Communication will be achieved via your armor's neural network."

"Good enough for me," Osiris said. "Ok, so how do we get to fight the Horsemen directly? We don't have time to go through the ranks."

"A challenge," Ronin said excitedly. "Once we ascend this monolith, we must each issue a challenge against the Clan Chiefs. They will be forced to accept. Unfortunately, challenges are typically only used to settle disputes and vendettas. We would be forfeiting the chance to lead the Warrior Guild."

"We're not here to run for bloody Prime Minister," Osiris said. "We will challenge them, get them to agree to help us, then get back to the Collective."

"Challenge matches are usually settled when one of the combatants dies or yields."

"Perfect..." Wayland huffed. "We can just yield and be on our way."

"No," Osiris said quickly. "You yield too soon, and the Clan Chief will not respect you as a warrior. Plead your case during your fight. Do not yield until they agree to help."

"What of our metallic friend?" Ronin said, looking over his shoulder. "I doubt they'll allow Auggie to take part in the Trials."

"Damn. I didn't think of that," Osiris said, pausing his efforts.

"I will remain in this form," Auggie said. "They will not detect that I am a droid."

"I dunno, Auggie. I'm sure they have some pretty sophisticated tech up there. Not detecting the comm devices I can see being probable, but an entire A.U.G. unit?! Doesn't seem possible."

"Um, guys, can we keep climbing? Kind of dying down here."

"I will not be detected. I have countermeasures in place to ensure I am not."

"I've never heard of a droid with such capabilities," Ronin said.

"There are not any droids that can," Auggie said. "Except for me. That is the reason I have stayed in this form since we made contact with the Warrior Guild. So they would not suspect. Our mission hinges on the fact that we do not get caught."

"What countermeasures?" Ronin asked suspiciously.

"I am very sorry, Guardian Magus. I am not at liberty to say."

"On whose authority?" Ronin asked, a little forcefully.

"Guys," Wayland grunted.

"I am sorry, Guardian Magus…"

"Forget it, Auggie. Ronin, mate, let's worry about that later, yeah?" Osiris asked beseechingly. "Aug, Alana trusts you. Max trusts you. I suppose I trust you, too. If you say you won't get caught, I believe you. Let's all just stay focused. We are nearing the top and…"

"Oh, there I go," Wayland exclaimed as the muscles in his arms and hands gave up. He fell backward in an almost reverse swan dive, his arms whirling in circles in an attempt to catch himself. "This is going to huuuurrrrrt!"

CHAPTER FIFTEEN

CYBER WARFARE

Max gazed up as they walked through the automated glass doors of the massive high-rise building. They took their dropship to the outskirts of the bustling city of Kyoto, only minutes ago, and now they were in the business district, inside a building owned by the Jisedai-Sen Studios. Sun Tzu told them that his daughter, Ayako, worked somewhere in the very building they were in. The lobby they stood in was open and expansive. The marble floors were highly polished and the walls were metallic. At varying intervals on the walls were posters of art and, what looked like to Max, videogame art. It was a strange combination. Max extended his attention to the people that hurried about in the lobby. People dressed in suits were actually outnumbered by people dressed in street clothes.

"This place is massive," Max said, as he spun around trying to take in all the sights. "What kind of company is Jisedai-Sen again?"

"Yes, it is massive," Charlotte agreed, as she looked around wide-eyed.

"Come," Alana said, as she walked to the receptionist's desk.

As they came upon the receptionist, Max saw a statue standing next to the counter of the reception area. It was a large figure wearing gleaming armor and holding a futuristic weapon. The statue was posed to look like he was calling to his compatriots to join the imaginary battle he was engaged in.

"Hey, that's a legionnaire from *Battleground Earth.*"

"Is that a book?" Alana asked.

"A video game," Max said suspiciously, as he spun around looking at his surroundings again with new eyes. "What's this company called again?"

"Jisedai-Sen Studios," Charlotte said. "It translates to Next Generation…"

"…Warfare," Max blurted, finishing her statement. "No freaking way!"

"I don't understand, Max."

"Alana, this is NGW Studios! They make some of the best MMO's and FPS games in the world."

"Sorry?"

"Video games, they make video games. Specifically, war video games," Max said excitedly.

"So, Ayako is a video game designer?" Alana said perplexed.

"Dunno, I guess," Max said grinning. "I wish we had time to tour this place. Wayland is going to be so jealous."

"Let me talk to the receptionist," Charlotte said.

Moments later, Charlotte returned. "He said that Ayako-san is currently in the company gym. He said that she is expecting us."

"To the gym," Max said excitedly. "And, walk slow, we might see some behind-the-scenes stuff!"

Alana just shook her head.

They took an elevator to the fourteenth floor of the building. When the doors opened, they saw that the entire floor was dedicated to exercise. Dozens of people, dressed in athletic gear, moved about the various weight and cardio machines. In the middle of the gym was a boxing ring. Max noticed two people sparring in the ring. They were both skilled fighters, but the smaller fighter was faster and seemed to be gaining the upper hand.

"Look at those two go," Max said impressed.

Charlotte and Alana looked at the fighters.

"Familiar," Charlotte said.

"Absolutely," Alana agreed.

"What's that now?" Max asked perplexed.

"That girl's fighting style," Alana said.

"She fights like the Ninjas of Iga," Charlotte mused.

"Ayako Kurosawa, I presume," Alana said.

"You can't possibly tell who someone is by how they fight," Max scoffed. "That's just crazy."

Alana and Charlotte began to walk towards the ring. Max moved quickly to catch up.

"Fighting is a conversation. You speak with your actions and movements. If you pay attention, each fighter has his or her own language. People who train together tend to speak that same language," Alana said, as they walked.

Max looked back at the fighters and tried to focus on their individual movements. Their bodies were a blur of action. As he stared, he began to notice… something. The angle of a kick. The position of a fist. He had seen these before… but he couldn't be sure. "I think I see what you're talking about. Kinda."

"Do not worry, Max," Charlotte said. "It becomes easier with practice."

As they reached the ring, the smaller fighter jumped up and spun twice in the air. On her last revolution, she flung her right foot out, performing a flawless outward crescent kick. The attack found its mark, as the other fighter's head was rocked to the side and he fell to the ground. The smaller fighter advanced on her fallen opponent, but the man raised his hand in submission.

"Good round," the lady said as she grabbed the man's hand and helped him up.

"That kick is too fast," the man said. "You get me every time," he laughed, rubbing his chin.

The lady took offer her sparring helmet. "It's only going to work for so long. Do not repeat the tactics that have gained you one victory, but let your methods be regulated by the infinite variety of circumstances."

"Why can't you ever just say, 'better luck next time'," the man laughed again. "See you back in the studio, Ayako. I'm going to go shower the smell of loser off in the locker room."

Ayako smiled. "It didn't work last time. Maybe you'll have better luck this time."

The man smiled and shook his head. "Yes, Sensei." He left the ring and walked past Max, Alana, and Charlotte.

Ayako saw them and greeted them by raising her chin slightly. "My dad said you would be coming, Charlie."

"Ayako," Charlotte said warmly. "I see you're still quite the fighter."

"Frank is from our Los Angeles offices. He's been taking MMA classes with that Earthborn fighter Cin Fargain. He thought with the new lessons he could finally beat me. Frank's a good guy, I don't have the heart to tell him that I'm barely breaking a sweat."

Charlotte smiled. "And you are as humble as ever."

"Don't start with me, Charlie. I already get it from Dad. Why do you think I moved to Kyoto?"

"Master Tzu only wants the best for you."

"As long as he gets to decide," Ayako said, as she put her helmet back on.

Charlotte simply nodded, trying to avoid a fight. "So, are you ready to depart? We have much to do back in the Collective."

"Charlie, I'm going to tell you what I told Dad. I'm not going anywhere. I can take care of myself."

"You seem fairly competent in the ring," Alana said, "but, you are not prepared for what The Fallen will do when they come after you."

"Fairly competent…" Ayako repeated incredulously. "I'm sorry, who are you?"

"Alana Anderson of the Order of Light."

"Oh, you're an Order chick. Ok, that makes sense."

"What is that supposed to mean?"

"You all think you're so elite. Nobody is as good as the Order," Ayako said in a mocking voice.

Alana's anger surfaced for a moment, but she wrestled it down, controlling herself. "We have come at your father's request. You will leave with us, even if I have to drag your spoiled butt out myself," she said calmly.

"Spoiled?! You don't even know me."

"We do not have time for a tantrum," Alana said. "We have a nation to save. Will you come willingly?"

Ayako smiled. "I like you. Because I like you, I'll make you a deal. You get in the ring with me and win, and I'll go with you, no questions asked. If I beat you, you run home and leave me the hell alone."

"Ayako, we're just trying to take care of you," Charlotte said pleadingly. "Why must you be so difficult?"

"You weren't the boss of me when we were kids, Charlie. And, you're not the boss of me now."

Charlotte rolled her eyes exasperated. "Always so dramatic."

"Deal," Alana said. "I'll even deactivate my armor so you feel like the fight is more even. I'll only leave the cloaking protocols in place."

"You're wearing armor?" Ayako asked distracted. "Wow, your cloaking software is good."

Alana jumped into the ring, clearing the ropes with ease. "Prepare yourself," she said, as she bowed.

Ayako took her helmet off and threw it to the side. "I'm not going to need that," she smiled. She bowed perfunctorily then raised her fists. "Come on, agent. Show me what you've got."

Alana jabbed quickly, tagging Ayako on the chin. She then stepped in and elbowed her in the stomach. Ayako doubled over and stepped a few feet back. Her cocky demeanor washed away only to be replaced with anger. Ayako threw a roundhouse kick to Alana's head, but Alana easily ducked under it. While Alana moved to a crouch, she tried to sweep Ayako's leg out from under her, but Ayako proved to be even faster than Alana thought. While still standing on one leg, mid-kick, Ayako jumped over Alana's sweep and heel hooked her in the head.

Max was instantly worried. He'd never seen Alana take a strong hit like that before. Alana, stunned for a second, shuffled back to regain her footing. Ayako jumped at her, attempting to perform the crescent kick that brought her victory with Frank only minutes ago.

Before Ayako finished her turns in the air, Alana jumped and superman punched Ayako in the face. The blow was perfectly timed, and the power of the punch knocked Ayako out cold.

"Founder bless us. Alana, you killed her," Charlotte said as she hurriedly got into the ring and knelt next to Ayako to check her vitals.

"Only knocked out," Alana said casually. "I placed the punch right below her temple. The damage will be minimal, but the force behind the punch was just enough to knock her out for few moments."

"Alana," Max said with a hint of fear in his voice. "Have I told you how lucky we are that you're on our side?"

Alana smiled. "Not today, no."

"We're lucky you're on our side."

"Yes. Yes, you are."

Ayako's eye's fluttered open. "What just happened?" she groaned.

"Alana just knocked you out," Charlotte said kindly.

Ayako sat up rubbing her head slightly. "Damn. I didn't see you coming."

"I am sorry, Ayako-san. But, we do not have time to dally. I had to end the fight quickly."

"Yeah, you definitely did that. Well, crap. This whole thing played out way differently in my head, but I guess a deal is a deal." She got up shakily, but refused Charlotte's help to exit the ring.

"I got it, I got it."

Ayako grabbed her gym bag. "How long are we going to be gone? I have a few deadlines I have to meet for work."

"Deadlines, for like video games, right?" Max asked excitedly.

"Who's this guy?" Ayako asked, wincing slightly at the pain she felt to talk.

"We'll explain everything on the ship," Alana said.

"So, are you a designer or something?" Max continued his query.

"Yeah. Lead design for Battleground Earth."

"You shut your face," Max said, as a huge smile spread across his face. "You shut your face right now!"

Ayako couldn't help but laugh a little. "Yeah. That's me."

"Let's move," Alana said, checking her gauntlet secretively.

She began to walk back to the elevator with everyone in tow. They entered and faced forward. The doors began to close when Max turned to Ayako excitedly and asked, "Do you think I could have your autograph?"

CHAPTER SIXTEEN

ROUND ONE, FIGHT

Wayland looked around in awe. From the moment they climbed over the ledge at the top of the butte, the sheer beauty and grandeur of the arena rendered him speechless.

They were being led to the inner sanctum of the arena, where they were going to be presented to the interim Battlemaster, Lady Sif Sekhmet. The sun had completely gone down and the night sky was ablaze with stars. The expansive arena was open air and was lit throughout with glowing blue orbs that floated several feet off the ground. The area was bathed with blue light, punctuated with orange-red from the various fires and torches that were lit sporadically.

As they walked, Wayland noticed that everyone around him laughed and greeted one another like old friends. If he hadn't known better, Wayland would say they were crashing some sort of party.

"I thought we weren't supposed to talk to each other?" Wayland whispered.

Ronin barked out a laugh. "Once the tournament begins, fighters will be brought to their own personal holding area. The spectators will then take their seats. Right now, it is a time for merriment. A time to reminisce of battles fought valiantly in the past with the hope of many more glorious battles to be fought in the future."

"Oh," Wayland said quietly. "I thought since you guys weren't talking, that the whole not talking thing started already."

"Wayland...," Osiris said, glancing sidelong at him.

"Yeah?"

"...You talk too much, mate," Osiris said, with a smirk.

"Lady Sif awaits you through there," the guide said to them.

The guide had waited for the boys at the top of the butte when they finally made it. This was the first time she talked to them since then.

"So, are you fighting today?" Wayland asked the guide clumsily. "Maybe afterwards we can hang out or something?"

The guide smiled. "Lady Sif awaits you through there." She turned and walked gracefully away.

"So, you'll think about it then?" Wayland called after her.

"Come on, Romeo," Osiris said, nudging Wayland to walk through the vaulted door that led to the inner sanctum.

"I think she's into me," Wayland said grinning.

The group walked in to the inner sanctum. Inside, the décor and furnishings were Spartan. Lady Sif sat on a wooden chair on a raised dais. Osiris led the group forward and bowed deeply in front of Sif.

"Osiris," she said flatly.

"My lady," Osiris said grinning.

"What are you doing here, lad?"

"We've come to test my mettle in the arena, against the greatest warriors this age has ever known." Osiris said.

"Don't," Sif said. "Your silk tongue has gotten you into much misfortune with our Guild before. Let's dispense with this charade and get down to why you're really here."

"You wound me, my lady," Osiris said, still grinning. "As you recall, that incident with Excalibur ended up working out for all of us. The sword is with its rightful owner, and we all got a little wealthier in the process. Win, win, right?"

Sif rolled her eyes. "Someday, your luck will run out. I would hate to see you end up on the wrong side of my blade," she said annoyed.

"Let's hope that day never comes, my lady."

"Enough of this," Sif said impatiently. She turned to Ronin. "Why are you and your friends here, First Knight of the Realm?"

Ronin bowed. He knew Sif and the rest of the Warrior Guild did not take well to idle chitchat. Why Osiris chose to vex the Lady Sif was beyond his comprehension. "My lady, Osiris Pendragon, Wayland Smith, and Aug..." Ronin paused. He realized that they never came up with a false name for Auggie. "Uh... Augustus Brutus, and I wish to represent our Houses in the arena."

"I see," Sif said nodding slowly.

"Didn't I just say that?" Osiris said quickly.

"Him, I believe," Sif said. "To what end, Ronin?"

"Glory and honor, my lady," Ronin said, as he bowed again.

"When I saw the request from Alastriona that four of her warriors be admitted in the Trials of Kratos, my suspicions were abound. Why would Alastriona send her finest warrior and the rest of you rabble?" Sif looked over at Viking Auggie. "Who are you again?"

Auggie looked at Ronin, then back at Sif. "Augustus Brutus," Auggie said in his mock accent.

Sif looked him over then shrugged. "Nice kirtle."

Auggie grunted his thanks.

"Fine. You want to fight. Let's play this out," Sif continued. "Is your House laying claim to the title of Battlemaster?"

"No, my lady," Ronin said quickly. "We wish to issue a challenge."

Sif stared at Ronin, squinting her eyes as she tried to read Ronin. "Go on," Sif said cautiously.

Ronin squared his shoulders. "We challenge the Four Horsemen of the Warrior Guild to single combat."

Sif guffawed. She laughed hard and long. "You wish... you wish to fight the Horsemen?" More laughter. "Actually fight them one-on-one?"

Ronin sighed, a little embarrassed. "Yes, my lady, we..."

Sif laughed even harder.

"Please, my lady..."

"Ahhh, I see now," Sif said, as her laughter subsided. "I didn't realize Alastriona and Plato were so desperate. They know I can't commit the Houses to battle, but if the four of you can convince the Clan Chiefs to fight, then you bypass our war councils." Sif wiped tears from her eyes as she finally stopped laughing. "A bold plan the two of them concocted, to be sure. Except they forget one simple fact."

"What might that be?" Osiris asked.

"The four of you will not survive," Sif grinned.

"Say what now?" Wayland asked.

ROUND ONE, FIGHT

* * *

Wayland sat in his holding area, on a bench against the wall. The front of his paddock was open, save for the force field that was in place. Wayland found out the hard way that he cannot pass through the field when he tried reaching out to touch it. His finger was still numb from the contact.

"Comm-link established," Auggie's voice said. Wayland looked around wildly. Auggie's voice sounded like he was right next to him, but he was alone in the cell.

"Aug," Wayland whispered. "Where are you?" he asked, as he leaned and put his ear to the wall closest to him.

"I am in my holding paddock," Auggie said.

"How can I hear you so good?"

"It's the bloody neural link, you git," Osiris voice said over the comm-link. "Remember?"

"Yeah, of course. I was just messing with you guys."

"Ronin, you there?" Osiris called out.

"I am," Ronin answered. His voice was calm and even. They could hear Ronin breathing evenly and deeply.

"You okay, Ronin?" Wayland asked.

"I am meditating. Visualizing my victory. One must decide to win a fight before it even begins."

"Oh..." Wayland said. "That's... that's what I was doing, too."

132

"Listen up, lads," Osiris said urgently. "Remember the plan. Get into the arena, fight, convince the Horsemen to join us, then either win or yield. ONLY after they agree to help, Wayland."

"I know that," Wayland said defensively.

"I will not yield. I am a Knight of the Sacred Realm. I will see this fight to its end. An end of my own design," Ronin said evenly.

"Fine. Just don't kill him and don't get killed," Osiris said.

"Understood."

The gathered crowd in the stands began to cheer. The arena was full of raucous spectators. They stomped on the ground as they yelled, and the walls of the holding cells rumbled and shook.

"Oh boy," Wayland said, as his anxiety level shot up.

"Alright, I'm up," Osiris said.

"Wait, already?" Wayland said panicked.

Osiris did not answer. Instead, Auggie's voice came over the comm. "Challenge bouts are fought first. It seems Lady Sif wants Osiris to be the first of our group to battle in the arena."

Wayland quickly moved to the force field wall at the front of his cell. From this vantage point, he could see the entire arena. Across from his cell, Wayland could see both Ronin and Viking Auggie in their own individual cells. "Hey guys," Wayland said as he waved at them. Auggie waved back, but Ronin sat cross-legged with his eyes closed, still deep in meditation.

In the arena, Osiris walked to the middle of the battleground. He raised a fist and turned, addressing the entire crowd of the arena. They cheered as they recognized him. Osiris was smiling broadly.

"They all seem to like him," Wayland said encouraged.

133

"Guardian Pendragon's travels have brought him in contact with most factions of the Atlantean people. He is well known by most, for better or worse," Auggie said.

"Osiris Pendragon of the House Bellum, son of Primus, son of Lilandra, has issued a challenge," an announcer's voice boomed across the stands.

The crowd's cheers escalated and reached a crescendo as another man took the field. He was lean and muscular. His brown skin was littered with scars from battles past. On his back was a dao broadsword. Osiris saw the man and laughed. The other man smiled and laughed as well.

"Lord Blanco, Clan Chief of the House Feikai, accepts the challenge," the announcer yelled.

Osiris and Blanco met in the middle of the field and hugged.

"Wait, what is happening?" Wayland yelled over the noise of the crowd.

"You needn't yell," Ronin said quietly. His voice came in clear and unobstructed through the neural comm-link.

"It seems Guardian Pendragon is friends with Lord Blanco of the House Feikai."

"Yeah, for sure," Wayland said. "Oz knows everyone."

Osiris clapped Blanco on the shoulder as he quickly talked to him in ancient Atlantean. Blanco's smile faded and he nodded solemnly. Blanco said something quickly, then Osiris shook his head and smiled.

Blanco put his hands to the side and shrugged.

Osiris looked at him for a moment, laughed, and then nodded.

They grasped each other's forearms and hugged once again.

"One round. Death, knockout, or submission," the announcer said. A gong rang somewhere in the arena and the two fighters took their positions opposite one another.

"Oh man, oh man, oh man. What the heck did they say?" Wayland said to himself. "Osiris, if you can hear me, be careful."

Osiris looked over at Wayland and smiled mischievously.

Wayland frowned in confusion.

The gong rang again and both fighters squared off. Lord Blanco held his sword high in the air and walked in a circle, acknowledging the crowd. The people screamed for their Clan Chief. Osiris just stood there, his swords still in their sheath. Osiris looked amused, but anxious to get the fight over with. He gestured for Blanco to hurry up. Blanco sheathed his sword then ran at Osiris.

"Watch out," Wayland yelled.

Osiris continued to stand there, not even assuming a fighting posture.

"Amusing," Ronin said.

Blanco jumped up, flipped, and brought his heel down on Osiris's head. Osiris fell back in a spectacular display.

"Oz!"

Osiris did not stir for a full minute. Blanco raised his hands up and addressed the crowd. The noise was deafening.

"Winner, by knockout, Lord Blanco of the House Feikai," the announcer said over the din.

Osiris came to. He rose very slowly, a large gash streamed thick red blood on his forehead. He wiped away the blood with the back of his hand. Blanco saw him rise, then he walked over and grabbed

Osiris's arm and lifted it high into the air. Again, the crowd went wild. Osiris and Blanco clasped each other on the shoulder and smiled.

"See you soon, old friend," Osiris's voice came over the comm.

Blanco smiled and nodded, then they departed the battleground.

"Well," Osiris said, as he went back to his paddock. "One thing's for sure - Lord Blanco still kicks harder than a shotgun blast."

"What the hell just happened?" Wayland said perplexed.

"House Feikai is with us," Osiris said. "Blanco agreed to help us before the match even started. He's an old friend who owes me a favor. Ah, damn, that cut hurts."

"So, why didn't you just yield then?"

"Blanco wanted to put on a show for the people. For fun."

"For fun?!" Wayland asked exasperated. "You said we still had to fight so the clans would respect us as warriors. You just stood there and got smashed in the head!"

"Yes. Still true. Except, I'm part of the Warrior Guild. My dad is Primus, former Battlemaster. So, they already respect me as a warrior," Osiris laughed. "I just took the hit so the people could see a little blood shed. This is the Warrior Guild after all."

"You people are nuts," Wayland said, as he sat back on his bench. "Certifiably, nuts! Gave me a freakin' heart attack."

Ronin and Osiris laughed.

CHAPTER SEVENTEEN

BAD NEWS

Max stood on the periphery of the interior of the dropship. He gazed out over the Pacific Ocean as they flew silently and undetected by any means that the Earthborn had at their disposal. The isolation in the middle of the ocean offered a rare and untenable gift – peace. At least, the illusion of peace, an illusion that would be shattered once they reached their destination. At the Collective, the stresses and worries of the inevitable attack would be at the forefront of everyone's mind. But there, in the vast expanse of the great body of water, those worries were only abstract concepts to be entertained at a later time.

Alana stood by his side, silently offering comfort and reassurance to him. Ayako and Charlotte sat closer to the front of the ship where they watched a television feed from one of the smart panels that made up the interior walls of the craft.

An urgent chime played on the display, and the television show the girls were watching was replaced with a newscaster from Beacon News.

"We are very sorry, ladies and gentlemen. We have breaking news. Large explosions in the Iga region of Japan just occurred only moments ago."

Max and Alana rushed over to the display and joined Charlotte and Ayako.

"Authorities from Kyoto are baffled at this point. The region seemed to be an uninhabited area of the mountain region. Some are saying the explosions are somehow linked to The History Bombings that have taken place in the recent past. Investigations are now underway. We will be tracking this story closely as it unfolds. I'm Linda Welz for Beacon News."

The newscast winked out and the television show that was playing resumed. Charlotte touched the corner of the display panel and the television feed turned off. The panel became transparent, the outside world visible once again.

Ayako pulled out her cell phone and punched her father's number in. "Answer," she said to herself.

Max and Alana exchanged a look, both fearing the worst.

"Answer," she said again, this time more vehemently.

Her breathing became more rapid. "Answer," her voice cracked. Tears began to stream down as a silent sob racked her body.

Charlotte moved close to her and put an arm around her. "I'm sure Master Tzu was not there when this happened."

"You don't know that, Charlie. You don't know that. How did they find my dad so fast? The Fallen, how did they know?"

"They must have had your father under surveillance for some time now," Alana said quietly.

"No, my dad would have known. He would have," Ayako said almost imploringly.

"As Charlotte said, he, in all probability, was not present during the attacks," Alana tried to sound confident.

"We have to go back," Ayako said urgently.

"We cannot," Alana said. "We are only moments from reaching the Collective. It is not safe to return to Iga. What if the bombings are just a trick to lure us out? The Fallen know the Order will investigate the possible death of an Ancient. All this could be an elaborate ruse."

"He's my dad!" Ayako yelled, as she stood. "Take me back!"

Alana stood her ground. "We have to get back to the Collective and begin our preparations for the assault on Lemuria. Your father might be on his way there as we speak. Until we have more definitive answers, our safest plan of action is to get back to the Collective."

Ayako stared daggers at Alana. Several awkward moments passed then Ayako shifted her gaze to Max. "My dad said we had to help you at all costs. He said the fate of the world was in your hands and we had to do our part to help you." Ayako sniffed and wiped the tears from her face with the back of her hand. "I'll go with you and honor my father's wishes. But, if we find out my dad didn't make it... If he died on that cursed mountain... I will blame you. He got involved in this stupid war because he believes in you; believes in what you represent. His death will be on your head, and after this is all said and done, you and I will settle up." Ayako strode past them to the back of the dropship where she pulled her duffle bag from a rack and started rummaging through it.

Max stood there dumbfounded. He didn't know how to react. Everything Ayako said was true. As soon as the newscast was complete, he was already blaming himself for what happened. He looked at Alana, his face contorted with guilt and grief. Alana's eyes were soft as she reached out to touch his arm.

She is upset. She did not mean any of that.

No, Alana. She's right. Too many people are getting hurt... because of me.

Max, you can't blame....

Alana grabbed the side of her head, her eyes shut tight.

"Alana, what's wrong?" Max said, grasping her shoulders to steady her. "Alana!"

"A push, from Master Plato," she said breathlessly, as she opened her eyes. "I wasn't expecting it, that's all."

"Is everything ok?" Charlotte asked, concern lacing her voice.

"No," Alana said faintly, as she looked off into the distance. Her gaze refocused and she looked at them. Max saw the genuine fear in her eyes. "The Tablet of Destiny has been stolen," she said. "The Fallen now control the Leviathan."

CHAPTER EIGHTEEN

ROUND TWO, FIGHT

Ronin drove his sword's tip in the sand of the arena and dropped to one knee, as he said a battle prayer quietly to himself. Even though the crowd cheered loudly around him, the prayer came through the comm-link to Osiris, Auggie, and Wayland loud and clear.

"Great Founder of this world. You, who forge courage and bravery, you, who tame the great forces of land, sky, and sea, lend me your strength on this day. Grant me fortitude, endurance, and the wisdom needed to be victorious on the field of battle. For this, I pray."

"Ronin Magus, First Knight of the Sacred Realm, and champion to Princess Charlotte of the Collective of Lemuria, has issued a challenge," the announcer boomed.

Ronin stood and placed both hands on the hilt of his sword waiting patiently for his opponent.

From the opposite side of the field, a large door opened and a thin man with flowing robes walked serenely out into the arena. He carried a long green staff in one hand that doubled as a walking stick. The crowd cheered, but it was different than it was for Lord Blanco. They were more reverent of the warrior taking the field.

"Lord Ventura, Clan Chief of the House Ariston, accepts the challenge," the announcer said. "One round. Death, knockout, or submission!"

The crowd quieted, as Lord Ventura kneeled in front of Ronin and placed his staff in front of him. Ronin pulled his sword from the sand, knelt, and placed his weapon in front of himself, as well.

"Aug, what's going on?" Wayland whispered, as the arena became deathly quiet.

"Lord Ventura is from the House Ariston. The clan is comprised of warrior-monks. To be Ariston is to adopt a life in service to the Founder," Auggie said quietly.

"Ariston starts their battles in prayer for themselves and their opponents," Osiris said. "Mighty thoughtful of them to pray for the people they are about to kill," he chuckled.

"Dude, not funny," Wayland said. "So, why is Ronin kneeling too?"

"Guardian Magus is respecting the Ariston ritual by taking part in it," Auggie said.

"I've been wondering, Aug, why do you call everybody a guardian?" Wayland asked.

"I do not call everyone a Guardian. Only the Guardians."

"Pipe down, you two. They are about to start," Osiris said rapidly.

Both men bowed to their weapons and then sat up straight. Ventura began to stand, but Ronin spoke, stopping the man.

"Lord Ventura, it lifts my spirits to see you again," he said smiling.

Ventura nodded and said something back to him. The comm-link could not broadcast what he was saying.

"You honor me," Ronin answered back. "Before we begin, I feel it my duty that I should tell you that I am here under false pretenses."

Ventura frowned slightly.

"I am here to ask a favor of you and your Clan, my lord."

Ventura nodded and gestured for Ronin to continue.

"The Collective of Lemuria, my home, is in dire need of you and your warriors. I have fought by your side in many skirmishes. We have trained together and now I come to you as a brother in arms. Please, help me defend my people against The Fallen. They mean to attack us, and, with them, a horde of would-be conquerors. Ariston has always been a House of honor and justice. The Fallen spit on these principles and seek only death and destruction. Will you help us, brother?"

"What the crap?" Wayland exclaimed. "Why is he asking Ventura before the fighting? Osiris, you said fight, then ask. Fight then ask."

"I guess we failed to mention that the Warrior Guild also knows Ronin. He's trained and fought with them before."

"Oh, I see, so that rule only applies to me then. Well, that's just great," Wayland said, as he threw up his hands.

"They do not know me either best-friend-Wayland. Do not worry."

"Ugh, you guys are killing me."

Ventura took a deep breath and a moment to think, then nodded. He stood and Ronin mirrored his friend. Ventura said something quickly and Ronin nodded.

"Yes, absolutely," he said. "I wouldn't have it any other way, and, thank you, old friend."

Ventura nodded again. The gong chimed ominously.

"So, are you going to stand there like Osiris did?" Wayland asked annoyed.

"I wouldn't dare," Ronin answered. The gong rang again and the fight commenced.

Ronin attacked with his bastard sword, lunging quickly with the tip of the blade. Ventura spun out of the way with minimal movement. His staff shot out like a bullet and tagged Ronin in the chest. The armor took the brunt of the blow, but the boys in their cells could hear Ronin's breath huff out.

Ronin parried the staff away with his sword and, in the same motion, rammed his shoulder into Ventura's chest. He tried to step away, but Ronin was too fast. His shoulder rammed hard into Ventura and he flew back a few feet. Ventura caught himself with his staff and he hovered impossibly above the ground with the support of only his weapon.

Ronin swiped at the staff with the intent of bringing Ventura back down to the ground, but Ventura used the force of Ronin's strike to propel the bow in a wide arc. Before Ventura landed on the ground, the end of his staff cracked Ronin on top of his head. Ronin stumbled, slightly dazed from the hit. Ventura followed up by jumping up and kicking Ronin in the chest. He kicked several times, all the while still in the air, and Ronin was sent flying back. He landed on his back with a thud and the crowd groaned, feeling sorry for Ronin and the pain he was enduring. Ronin coughed up a little blood as he struggled to stand.

"Why doesn't he just use his telekinesis and throw him into a wall or something?" Wayland asked, wincing from seeing Ronin in pain.

"Against the rules," Osiris said hurriedly. "Just watch."

Ronin gathered himself and stood up, to the delight of the crowd. He grabbed the hilt of his sword with two hands and performed a powerful overhead slice. Ventura saw the attack coming from a mile away and began to move to the side to avoid the devastating but slow attack. Ronin quickly shifted his weight to his rear leg and spun on the spot. His free leg lashed out like an angry snake and caught Ventura on the chin. The feint had worked and now Ventura was lying on the ground.

Ronin lifted his sword so its tip was pointed at Ventura. "Do you yield, brother?"

Ventura looked up, blood smeared across his face, and he smiled. He stood and bowed to Ronin, and then he walked off the field. Ronin raised his fist in victory and the crowd boomed their approval.

CHAPTER NINETEEN

SEEDS OF DOUBT

Simon punched in a few commands onto his tablet. An inventory list was displayed and he began scrutinizing it, checking, and double-checking. From his vantage point on the terrace, Simon could oversee the entire staging operation. Thus far, everything was on schedule. Troops were being outfitted with armor and weapons and the armaments were being placed on the dropships and other larger cargo transports. War preparations were far more tedious than Simon could have ever imagined. The communicator on his wrist emanated a soft tone. Simon sighed. He knew all too well who was calling. The man had been a supreme annoyance ever since he joined the ranks of The Enlightened. Oddly, Simon had grown accustomed to having Primus as his commander. The pressures of being in charge was lifted when Primus came. Now, all he had to do was follow orders. Simon placed the tablet on the table next to him then pressed a button on the communicator. When he turned his palm upward, a small projection of Primus manifested a few inches from his hand.

"Praetor," Simon said flatly.

"Simon. How go the preparations?"

"On schedule. The Goliath-class transports are prepped and ready for launch and all Phantom dropships will be fully armed before close of business today."

"Well done, Simon. Well done, indeed. What of the attack on Iga?"

Simon looked away from the projection for a moment. Gathering his thoughts. "The attack was successful. The strike team decimated Tzu's village. We are coordinating with Earthborn authorities to recover Tzu's body and those of his students, as well."

"So, their bodies have not been found yet?"

"Not yet, Praetor."

"Mmm... Very well. Report to me once investigations are complete."

"Yes, Praetor."

"It is time for you to report back to headquarters. Malus is ready to commence with the experiments."

"The remaining Tablet has been recovered?" Simon's attention peaked.

"Indeed. The spy within the Collective proved to be useful."

"So... do we still plan to proceed with the attack on Lemuria?"

It was Primus's turn to look away, deep in thought. "It is... Lord Malus's wish is that we proceed according to plan."

"I don't understand, Praetor. We could save the troops for another more necessary battle. All of our resources have been poured into this operation. Would it not be a waste of time?"

Primus arced an eyebrow as he studied Simon. "This is Lord Malus's will. Follow orders, Simon. Report to headquarters. I will deal with the deployment of our troops from this point forward."

Simon frowned, but nodded his compliance. "Yes, Praetor."

CHAPTER TWENTY

ROUND THREE, FIGHT

Viking Auggie lumbered into the arena from his holding cell. He stopped briefly to scratch his backside before he reached the center of the ring.

"Auggie," Ronin queried. "What reason would you have to scratch your behind?"

"Little nuances give the appearance that I am, in fact, an Organic," Auggie said over the comm-link.

"An Organic?" Wayland asked.

"It is what my kind calls your kind," Auggie said.

"Hmm, makes sense," Wayland mused. "So, what do we do Oz? No one in the Guild knows who Auggie is. Me neither for that matter. How do we win?"

"We go with the original plan," Osiris answered. "Auggie, you know what needs to be done. Do not kill him."

"Yes, Guardian Pendragon."

"Augustus Brutus of the Ferrum Clan has issued a challenge," the announcer said, sounding a little confused. "Why is the Craft Guild here?" he said to someone in the announcer's booth, away from the microphone he was using."

"Great name by the way," Wayland said sarcastically.

"It is doubtful you would have thought of something better under such pressure," Ronin spat.

"Lord Blanco, Clan Chief of the House Bellum, accepts the challenge. One round. Death, knockout, or submission."

"Another Blanco?" Wayland asked.

"Yes, the Blanco brothers hail from this region. They are among the greatest warriors in the Guild," Ronin informed, studying the other Blanco brother as he took the field.

Lord Blanco of Bellum strode onto the field. He was heavily muscled and stout. The man walked with the confidence of someone who knew, unequivocally, how powerful he was.

The gong rang and Viking Auggie and Lord Blanco faced off.

"No weapon," Osiris observed.

"No," Ronin answered. "He prefers to utilize Awaten Ju Jutsu, empty hand combat. Notice his gauntlets?"

Blanco brought his metal encased fists together and the clang rang throughout the arena like a hammer hitting an anvil.

"Aug, buddy, be careful," Wayland said.

"Never fear, best-friend-Wayland."

The gong rang a second time and the fight began.

Blanco shifted forward, his metal studded hand shooting out like a missile. The blur of motion was almost impossible to perceive. Auggie's positronic brain, equipped with the latest in quantum processors, analyzed the move and made the appropriate decisions in a matter of milliseconds. Even with lightning fast technology on his side, Blanco's fist of steel still managed to scrape along Auggie's torso. The projection Auggie was using to mask his identity was only that, a projection. Any contact would reveal that his body was, in fact, metal. Blanco paused a moment, perplexed, when he saw sparks fly from his fist, as it made contact with Auggie's chest. Auggie didn't give him too much time to analyze what just happened. He brought his battle-ax down in a swift arc, slicing at Blanco's forearm. The ax glanced off the gauntlet, not inflicting any visible damage.

Blanco spun away, distancing himself from any further attacks. He smirked and said something to Auggie. Auggie held up his battle-ax and said, "This ax is made of orichalcum as well, Lord Blanco."

Blanco's smile faded as he inspected his gauntlet. He frowned in disbelief as he saw a fine cut in the metal casing. His frown turned into a snarl as he attacked Auggie again. Blanco threw punch after punch in a whirlwind of attacks. Auggie dodged and blocked most of the hits. A few times, one of Blanco's punches was met with Auggie's shield and the metal-on-metal sound reverberated around the arena. The crowd was beside themselves.

"Oz, how much damage can Auggie's shield take?" Wayland asked worriedly.

"A lot," Osiris said.

"I plan on wearing out Lord Blanco. Once he is exhausted, I will inflict minimal damage," Auggie said flatly.

"No talking, Aug," Osiris said. "Blanco will know you're communicating with someone."

"I'm not utilizing my voice synthesizer to speak to you," Auggie said. I can manifest voice patterns and transmit them silently on this comm-link."

"Oh…" Osiris said. "Ok, um… as you were then."

Blanco continued his mass attack, but he was becoming frustrated. Auggie scanned Blanco.

"Respiratory levels are at their peak. Heart rate elevated to maximum," Auggie said. "I believe Lord Blanco is reaching his physical boundaries."

Blanco spun, performing a heel hook kick, but Auggie leaned backward to avoid it. His head only bent back a few inches, so Blanco's foot was alarmingly close to his face. Sand from the arena floor trailed behind Blanco's foot, flying into the simulated eyes of Auggie's Viking. Auggie staggered back, rubbing at his eyes.

"Auggie, what are you doing?" Ronin bellowed. "The sand can't hurt you."

"I must maintain the illusion that I am an Organic," Auggie said, as he continued to feign the inability to see.

Blanco capitalized on Auggie's pseudo-blindness. He spun low and swept Auggie's legs out from under him, making Auggie hang in the air almost vertically for a split second. Blanco continued his spin and delivered a palm strike center mass of Auggie's chest sending him flying back.

Auggie lay still for a second.

"Auggie!" Wayland yelled.

Blanco walked forward breathing hard from all the exertion of the fight. He reached down to finish Auggie off. In one swift motion Auggie grabbed his wrist and locked his legs around Blanco's arm, causing the Clan Chief to fall to the ground. Auggie shifted his waist forward pressing on the elbow of Blanco's arm. He yelled in pain from the pressure of the arm bar. Auggie paused, waiting for Blanco to submit.

"Do you wish to yield, Lord Blanco?" Auggie asked politely.

Blanco shook his head violently. "Very well," Auggie responded. He pulled back on Blanco's arm again; this time, the appendage gave way to the pressure. A loud crack reverberated across the arena and the crowed hushed. Blanco grunted in pain as his radial bone snapped in two.

"Oh... look, there's his bo..." Wayland said woozily, as he fell over and fainted.

CHAPTER TWENTY-ONE

WRENCH'S NEW TOY

Wrench weaved through the crowd that was in front of the palace's portcullis. It was market day and many vendors from the city set up booths and stands to sell their wares. The queen carried on the medieval tradition of market day so they would always remember where they came from. On this day, it also offered a sense of normalcy in the face of uncertain times.

The news of the theft of the Tablet of Destiny traveled through Lemuria like a wild fire. Citizens were on edge, and rightly so. Never, in the history of Lemuria, had a crime of this magnitude ever taken place. Petty theft was one thing, but to break into the royal palace and steal from the queen herself was something entirely different.

Wrench eventually made his way to the palace gates. Heavily armored guards formed a barrier blocking the way. It was a departure from the detail of only two guards that typically guarded the entrance. A testament to the city's new posture of alertness. The guards saw Wrench running towards them and they leveled their weapons at him.

"Halt!" the lead guard bellowed.

"I have news…" Wrench wheezed, holding up a work tablet. "News for the queen."

Wrench kept running forward and the guard yelled again,

"Halt!"

Wrench was confused. He was the chief engineer for the geothermal plant. He was supposed to be allowed access to speak with the queen whenever he wanted. He never utilized this right, but still, it was his right. Wrench continued running forward. "I am Chief Engineer of the…"

Wrench ran right into a force field that was surrounding the palace. If he had been paying attention, he would have noticed the signs posted stating that the defensive barrier was operational. He also might have noticed the guard's face when he was yelling 'halt'. It was a face of concern, not aggression. Wrench fell back, the front of his body going instantly numb. The guard ran to him, deactivating the barrier as he did.

"You alright, Wrench?" the guard asked.

"Ooohh gnow muh gname?" Wrench asked, his face and tongue numb from the field.

The guard laughed. "Yes, I know your name. You're the guy who keeps Lemuria's power running. We all know who you are."

"Uh, dint gnow uh wa famoh." Wrench tried to smile.

"Yeah," the guard laughed again. "Famous." The guard grabbed him by the arm and helped him up. "Up you go."

"Kank ooo. Uh gotta shee ga keen. Ruhee ingorcant."

"Alright. Really important. Trackin'. I'll take you up to see her. Come on."

The guard led Wrench to the meeting room in the inner chamber of the palace. As Wrench walked through, he noticed a large holographic display of a map hovering over the large circular table of the meeting room. On the boundaries of the room, people sitting at makeshift workstations worked vigorously at their tasks.

"My Queen," the guard announced.

Alastriona looked up. "Yes, Captain Evans, what is it?"

"Chief Engineer Braxis to see you, Your Majesty."

Alastriona looked at Wrench and smiled, recognizing the strange, but brilliant young man. "Thank you, Captain."

Evans bowed and left the room. "Wrench, isn't it?"

Wrench smiled. The numbness of the force field had thankfully faded. "Yes, My Queen. That's what my friends call me."

Alastriona smiled. "How can we help you, Wrench? As you can see, we have much to do today."

"Yes, of course you do," Wrench said giggling slightly. "I'm sorry, I've just never been in the palace before... it's so cool."

Plato and Lady Sotera looked up from the plans they were going over. Wrench saw Sotera and a look of pure joy came across his face.

"Holy lava cakes..." Wrench said, his eyes glued to Sotera. "It's you. Lady Sotera. Clan Chief of the House Ferrum. Master Armorer for the Order of Light. Hero of the Cryptid Wars!" Wrench rattled off the stats like a fan boy would of their favorite superhero.

Sotera smiled. "Aye, lad. That's me."

Wrench smacked a technician on the shoulder. "It's her," he said excitedly. "Oh, best day ever. I've read everything about you, ever since I came to this city. You make the best stuff. You're a genius."

"I like this boy," Sotera said quietly to Plato, who smiled in turn.

Alastriona, somewhat annoyed, cleared her throat. "Wrench... you needed to tell *me* something?"

"Huh? Oh... yeah. For sure." Wrench walked over to the table that they were all standing around. As he did, Wrench stole a glance at Sotera and waved. Sotera chuckled to herself and shook her head. "Yes, Your Majesty. I think I know how to solve your problem."

"There are several problems we are facing right now, Wrench. To which are you referring to?" Plato asked kindly.

"Oh, hey, Master Plato. There ya are. The Plato..." Wrench giggled nervously again. "Sweet." Wrench shook his head berating himself under his breath. "Be cool, Wrench. Be cool." He looked up at Alastriona. "Yes. Your problem. Um... give me just a sec..." Wrench powered his tablet on.

He tapped into the network of the palace and uploaded his tablet's operating system into the mainframes that were powering the meeting room's computers. He flicked the image on his tablet towards the holographic display above the table and the map that was hovering over the table disappeared, replaced with a schematic of the Leviathan.

"That problem," Wrench said proudly. "I know how we can beat it."

"How did you hack our system?" a technician demanded, as he stood up staring at the image of the Leviathan.

"Oh, it's pretty easy. See, all you have to do is..."

"Wrench," Alastriona cut in. "Where did you get these schematics?"

"Down in the lab, at the power plant."

"What lab?"

"Oh, it's the coolest. There's a secret lab down there. I found it one day while I was playing hide-and-seek with the ladies."

Alastriona looked at Plato. "I have no memory of such a lab," she said to him.

Plato shook his head slowly. "I've never heard of a lab in the power plant either."

"Yeah, it's totally down there. There are all kinds of things down there. Like these schematics for the Leviathan. And, that brings me to the solution to your problem." Wrench swiped on a new image on his tablet and the Leviathan was replaced with a new schematic - the drawing depicted a large robot. "Boom!" Wrench said proudly. "*This* is down there, too!"

"It can't be," Plato said astounded.

Alastriona slowly grabbed for her chair; her gaze fixed on the hovering image. "Is that... a Titan?

CHAPTER TWENTY-TWO

FINAL ROUND, FIGHT

The announcer sounded flustered. The emergence of Lord Mitchell onto the battleground was out of order. The announcer didn't have the opportunity to announce the next fight. Instead, he was now floundering in the booth, while the Clan Chief waited impatiently. The man's large frame seemed to dominate the arena. Tattoos ran across his entire body. Atlantean glyphs retelling the tales of the battles and wars Lord Mitchell had been involved in. His hair was shaved down to the scalp, which revealed a large scar that seemed to run directly down the center of his scalp from front to back. In his hand, he carried an oversized battle hammer that looked to be the size of an anvil.

"Uh… Lord Mitchell, Clan Chief of the House Senso, accepts the challenge of uh…Wayland Smith, of the House Ferrum."

"Get on with it," Mitchell bellowed to the announcer's booth.

"Yes, uh…one round. Death, knockout, or submission," the announcer finished.

Mitchell pointed at Wayland. "Death," Mitchell yelled.

The force field of Wayland's cell opened up. Wayland stayed where he was. The crowd began to laugh at Wayland's hesitation.

"Get out there, Wayland," Osiris urged over the comm-link. "How are you supposed to impress the Warrior Guild if you act like a coward?"

"This dude's crazy," Wayland said shakily.

"Come, friend Wayland. You have faced mightier opponents. Show Lord Mitchell the mettle with which you are forged from," Ronin said encouragingly.

Wayland tentatively stepped out of his cell. "I hate you guys," he whispered.

When he made it onto the battleground, the crowd's laughing and jeering almost completely went silent. Wayland's sheer mass made everyone stare at him in disbelief. As large as Lord Mitchell was, Wayland towered over him.

Mitchell looked him over. "You're a big one, aren't you?"

"Yes, sir, lord, sir," Wayland said nervously.

Mitchell laughed and raised his hammer into the air. The crowd cheered for their fighter.

Wayland looked over at his friends. "Okay, guys, what do I do?"

The gong rang.

"Best-friend-Wayland, Lord Mitchell means to end your life-force. You should be very afraid for your life," Auggie said earnestly.

"What?!"

The gong was struck again and immediately Mitchell swung his mighty hammer, catching Wayland under the chin. Wayland flew back nearly 20 feet and skidded to a halt in the sand. The crowd hushed. In their eyes, no one could take a hit like that and survive. The attack was so sudden, so violent, that no one knew how to react.

Wayland stood up quickly rubbing his chin. "Ow," he groaned.

The crowd burst into applause and cheers. Wayland survived a direct hit from the Horseman that was nicknamed Death. Mitchell crushed all enemies before him, but there was Wayland. Standing. Seemingly unharmed. Mitchell let out a war cry and charged at Wayland.

"Best-friend-Wayland, he is still trying to kill you."

Wayland stopped rubbing his chin and looked up. He yelped in surprise and began to run away.

"No, don't run," Osiris said frustrated. "Stand your ground."

"*You* stand your ground," Wayland yelled. "This maniac is after *me!*"

Wayland reached the end of the arena and he turned to continue his retreat. Mitchell caught up and raised his hammer for another strike. Wayland flailed his arms wildly, trying to get around Mitchell and, as he did, his elbow struck Mitchell in the nose. Mitchell staggered back with his hand over his face. When he pulled his hand away, the crowd caught sight of the blood that was now streaming freely from his nose.

The crowd gasped in response.

"I'm so sorry, Chief Lord Mitchell, sir. I didn't mean it."

"Nobody makes me bleed my own blood!" Mitchell thundered.

"Argh!" Wayland screamed and began running again.

Mitchell threw his hammer and it struck full force on Wayland's back. Wayland fell forward, his face digging into the ground.

"Up, Wayland. Get up," Ronin urged.

Wayland turned over, just in time to see Mitchell crashing down on him like a boulder. The force of Mitchell's body mass falling onto him crushed the wind out of Wayland. He huffed in pain. Mitchell proceeded to rain blow after blow down on Wayland's face. Mitchell was laughing maniacally as each fist found their mark.

"Make…" Wayland said in between hits.

"…Him…" Crunch.

"…Stop." Whack.

"If he maintains that position much longer, he will kill you," Auggie said matter-of-factly.

Wayland yelled and pushed Mitchell off of him with all of his strength. Mitchell flew back, but he rolled backwards, minimizing the force of the fall. Like an angry bull, Mitchell came charging back at Wayland. Scrambling back, Wayland's hand came into contact with the handle of Mitchell's war hammer. In a panic, Wayland hefted the hammer and threw it at Mitchell. It was an unexpected move, and the flying hammer caught Mitchell squarely in the face. The force of the blow lifted Mitchell off of the ground and he fell back. He landed squarely on his back, completely knocked out.

"Woo-hoo!" Osiris whooped, causing everyone on the comm-link to wince from the noise. "You did it, you giant fool! You did it!"

The crowd cheered, as Wayland laid back down, exhausted from the whole ordeal. "I really hate you guys," he rasped.

CHAPTER TWENTY-THREE

THE DRUMS OF WAR

Max sat at the table of the meeting room in the palace of Lemuria. The room had been converted into a make shift war room. He sat staring at the holographic image of some kind of robot. Its image rotated continuously, affording viewers a 360 degree view of the machine.

Alana and Charlotte sat together talking, while Ayako worked on her tablet. She frowned in concentration as she manipulated the images on the tablet.

Alastriona, Plato, Sotera, Jack, and Lara walked into the room. Everyone in the room stood up out of deference for the queen. "Please, everyone, no time for ceremony in times like these."

Ayako looked up and saw Plato. She searched the man's face.

"Nothing yet, Ayako-san," Plato said softly. "Which is a good thing. Our teams haven't found anything at the site of the attack. It is quite probable that Master Tzu escaped with his students."

Ayako nodded and resumed her work on the tablet.

Jack and Lara sat with Max, hugging him.

"So glad you're back safe," Lara said happily.

"You did well, Max," Jack said, patting him on the back. "I doubt Master Tzu would have agreed to help if anyone else but you went to talk with him."

"Actually, it was Charlotte and Alana. I just told him our story."

"I'm glad you're all home safe," Jack said, smiling at Alana and Charlotte, who returned his smile.

From the entrance of the war room a rowdy group joined them. "The conquering heroes return," Osiris announced.

Max smiled and ran over to his friends.

"Welcome back, you guys," he said, as he hugged each of them in turn. "Way… to hard, bro. Too hard."

"We come victorious from battle," Ronin said, proudly as he hugged Charlotte.

"I'm so glad you're home, my love."

"Every time with you two," Osiris said, as he shook his head. "Get a room."

Plato walked over to them and smiled broadly. "I'm glad you're all safe. I received your preliminary reports, Osiris. Your methods seemed a bit unorthodox, but I must concede to your results."

"That's why you hired me, Master. Results," Osiris said happily.

Plato clapped him on the shoulder. "Indeed, Oz. Come, all of you, sit."

They all sat at the round table. Plato stood and smiled. He looked at each of them individually before he spoke. "It does my heart good to see all of you gathered here together. While we still await the arrival of Master Tzu, we must continue with our preparations for the coming attack." Plato looked at Ayako to gauge her emotional state, but she was still engrossed with her work. "Thanks to… what did you call yourselves, Oz?"

"Team Alpha," Osiris said quickly.

Max, Alana, and Charlotte groaned with disapproval.

"Um, thanks to the efforts of Team Alpha," Plato continued, "the four clans of the Warrior Guild have agreed to aid Lemuria in its time of need. All of the agents from the Order have been called here, as well, for added assistance."

"What of the people of Lemuria?" Charlotte asked. "Do we have an evacuation plan in place?"

"We do," Alastriona said. "Some of our citizens have chosen to leave the Collective."

Max could almost hear Charlotte's heart breaking at the mention of her people leaving the Sacred Realm. "I... see," she said morosely.

"They must do what they feel is best for themselves and their families. We bear them no ill will. They will be welcomed back with open arms once this ordeal is behind us," Alastriona said sagely.

"Yes, of course," Charlotte agreed.

"Those who wish to stay have volunteered to fight with us and those who cannot fight will go into the chambers below the mountain that make up the Great Library," Plato said. "Librarian Vidya has been surprisingly accommodating."

Osiris raised his hand. "Hang on, you said some of the citizens of Lemuria are going to stay and fight? I appreciate their bravery, but The Fallen will cut through them like paper. Do you honestly think this rabble can defend the mountain?"

Sotera was fingering the shaft of her smith's hammer. "The people are steel," she said without looking up from her tool. "Forge and sharpen them. They will hold." She lifted her hammer and brought it down firmly on the table.

"Yes," Plato agreed. "This is their home. They will not be denied the opportunity to defend it."

Everyone in the room nodded quietly.

"I've also had a meeting with a small group of Casters, who have decided to lend their remarkable abilities to our cause. They will be imbedded with the different battalions in our force. Their magic will be invaluable in confusing the enemy."

"Did he just say magic?" Wayland asked to no one in particular. He looked over at Max who just shrugged.

"The Primordials that reside on this mountain have also agreed to help. So, as you can see, we have a formidable force."

"It won't matter," Ayako said, as she worked her tablet.

"I'm sorry, my dear?" Plato asked.

"It won't work," she repeated flatly.

"Are you saying our forces are not up to the task?" Ronin asked, his voice stern with controlled anger.

"No. I'm saying, unless you deploy your forces properly, The Fallen's army will still beat you. It's a simple numbers game."

"Who is this girl?" Ronin asked. "This is a war council. We should not have civilians present," he appealed to Plato.

Ayako put her tablet down and stood up. She pressed a button on the device and the map of Mt. Rainer blazed into existence in the holo-display in front of them. The map was superimposed over the structure that comprised the entirety of the Collective of Lemuria.

"You will be fighting on several fronts. If I were to attack, I'd hit you from all sides; spread your forces thin," Ayako said, contemplatively as she scanned the battle plans. "It won't matter how skilled your warriors are. Overwhelming numbers will always win out."

"What do you suggest?" Plato asked.

"Simple," Ayako said. "We need to even the playing field."

Ronin nodded as he studied the map. "What is your name, girl?"

"I am Ayako Kurosawa, daughter of Sun Tzu."

"And you believe yourself to be a suitable replacement for Master Tzu, simply because of your heritage?"

"Well, as far as strategists go, I'm probably the best trained person in this room. Unless you got some war general hidden in your back pocket, blondie, I'm all you got."

"Heh. Blondie. I like this girl," Osiris said, as he chomped on an apple.

"Please, Ronin," Alastriona said calmly. "If Ayako-san wants to try to help, I believe we should give her the opportunity. Allies are something we could always use more of. Besides, Ayako and Charlotte are old friends."

Ronin bowed his head swiftly. "Of course, My Queen."

"I'm here because my father wanted me here," Ayako said, loud enough so everyone could hear her. "I didn't choose to be here. But, I told my dad I would help *him*." She leveled a finger to Max. "I'm going to keep my word, then I'm out."

Plato nodded his head. "Understandable, Ayako."

"Fine… good," Ayako said tentatively. She was expecting an argument, but when none came, she didn't quite know how to proceed.

"So, what would you do to defend the mountain?" Plato prompted.

Ayako picked up her tablet and swiped several documents and pictures to the holo-display. "I've been going over your entire inventory and all of your vulnerabilities and weaknesses. Based on your past security breach, we have to assume the spy knows all these vulnerabilities and weaknesses, as well. If the spy knows, the enemy knows. So, the best way to proceed is to act as our enemies might. How would we attack ourselves?"

Ayako brought up a view of the mountain with two points marked on the map. "As far as I can see, you have two entry points to this city. Well, three, if you count the top of the mountain, but I think your laser grid covers that fairly well. The main entrance is located in a rock corral, easily defendable because enemy forces will be forced to bottleneck, leaving minimal room for any vehicles. The shields will hold against any projectiles, but if they deploy any field disrupters, we will have a hell of a time weathering a constant barrage from any of their long-range weapons. I propose we leave a small decoy force at the entrance to draw their fire, then take two separate forces and sneak up on their flanks. Once we've weakened them enough, the remaining force will move forward for clean up duty."

Max leaned over to Wayland. "She's the lead designer for Battleground Earth," Max whispered.

Wayland's eyes widened. "No freaking way! No wonder she knows so much about fighting wars and stuff."

"Right?!"

"Pay attention," Alana admonished.

"Sorry," they said in unison.

"Our forces on the back entrance should deploy guerilla warfare tactics. Set land mines, small skirmishes, that sort of thing. A head-on fight will give the advantage to the larger force. The control of a large force is merely a question of dividing up their numbers."

Ayako stopped talking and looked around the room. "Any questions so far?" No one said anything. "Blondie?"

Ronin smiled. He was not an overly prideful man, nor was he above admitting when he was wrong. "No, Ayako-san. Please continue."

Ayako allowed herself a small grin. "Ok, that brings us to the front entrance." The map shifted and a 3D topographical map of the other side of the mountain came into focus. "Here is where things can get difficult." The map moved across the expansive open area that made up the front side of the mountain. "As you can see, this is a wide open killing ground. We do not have the resources to maintain control of such a large area."

"More guerilla tactics?" Alana asked.

"Yes and no," Ayako said, as she highlighted a perimeter area around the front entrance. "We have to impose our will on the enemy first. If they set the tempo, we could be in for a long-drawn-out siege. Since we won't have any natural or artificial barriers available to us, we have to create the illusion of a barrier."

"Holographic displays?" Charlotte asked.

"Right train of thought, but I was thinking of something a little more practical," Ayako said, as she brought up another image on the holo-display.

Floating in front of them was what looked, to Max, like a hybrid between a fighter jet and a Transformer. "In your inventory, Your Majesty, you have a squadron of these little beauties."

"What in Founder's name are those?" Alastriona said. "I never approved a budget for that."

"Sorry, that's my bad," Wrench said from the corner of the room.

"Where the bloody hell you come from?" Osiris said startled.

"Sorry, I'm quiet like a ninja," Wrench said. "The name's Wrench."

"Wrench is welcome here," Sotera said.

Wrench elbowed Ronin in the side, "Isn't she the coolest? Oh, hey!" Wrench said, as he recognized whom he was standing next to.

Alastriona sighed, "Please, Wrench, let's stay on task."

Wrench's attention snapped back to the queen. "Yes. Sorry. So, yeah. Those are S.P.R.T.N.S or you can just say 'Spartans'; whatever floats your boat. They are Single Piloted Reconnaissance and Tactical Neuro-Suits that I designed for security purposes. I took the budget Queen Alastriona gave me to maintain the geothermal reactor and used it to design and build them."

"Then what money are you using to maintain the reactor?" Alastriona asked, doing all she could to hold back her frustration.

"Oh, that thing takes next to nothing to run. Ever since I recalibrated the systems and added a few modifications, that baby purrs like a kitten."

"Why didn't you tell me?" Alastriona asked through gritted teeth.

"Then where would have I gotten the money to build the Spartans?" Wrench asked confused.

"Never mind, Wrench, never mind. We can talk about that later," Alastriona said, brushing the question aside. "Ayako, how do you plan on deploying our... Spartans." She cast a side-ways glance at Wrench.

"I want to split the squadron into two forces. The first group will lie in wait on the outskirts of the forest of Rainer. When the main body of the enemy is in this area..." Ayako highlighted the center of the area just outside the perimeter of the front entrance, "...we will deploy the Spartans and begin bombing runs at the rear of their force."

"Creating our illusion of barriers," Charlotte said, comprehending what Ayako had in mind.

"Exactly. We create a 'firewall' all around them. They will instinctively move forward and away from the bombings, but into our inner perimeter where we can use the guerilla tactics you were talking about, Alana, to thin their numbers. I'm thinking land mines, snipers, Caster magic, the works. The battalions offered by the Warrior Guild and the remaining Spartans will then move out during the confusion and finish off what is left of the enemy. My only concern at this point is the eastern sector. The dense forest should offer us descent stand off, but it's an unknown quantity. I don't like unknowns."

"Amazing plan, love, really it is," Osiris said, leaning forward on the table. "But, how do we know The Fallen are still going to attack? They have the damn tablet. Why bother with the Collective now?"

"They are still coming," Plato sighed. "Our operative inside The Fallen confirmed that the attack is still a go."

"Unbelievable," Osiris said, as he sat back in his chair again. "There's no pleasing those people. Ok, so let's address the elephant in the room. How do we stop the bleeding Leviathan then?"

Ayako smirked. "With this."

She tapped her tablet and the massive form of a humanoid robot hovered before them in the holo-display.

"Looks like Voltron," Wayland whispered.

"Brother," Auggie said quietly, as he gazed at the Titan.

"That is a Titan," Plato said.

"Remember," Wrench said excitedly, "that's the cool thing I wanted to show you and Alana," he said, looking at Max.

"Oh... well, yeah, I'd say that's pretty cool," Max said, staring in awe at the machine.

"What's its purpose?" Ronin asked.

"It was built thousands of years ago for a single purpose - To defeat the Leviathan," Plato replied.

CHAPTER TWENTY-FOUR

DEPLOY

Simon stood next to Primus on the veranda. The assembled army was formed up in neat straight lines, prepared for inspection. Primus looked over the soldiers with a practiced eye.

"Everything looks in order," said Primus evenly.

"Thank you, Praetor," Simon said.

"I believe Lord Malus will be very pleased."

A beeping sound on the console in front of them demanded their attention.

"Ah, speak of the devil," Primus said, as he pressed the button.

From the veranda, a digital projection shot out in front of the assembled group. The light assembled and soon a 3D image of a man standing over 20 feet tall loomed over them. His dark cloak billowed around him and his face was hidden in darkness deep within his hood.

Lord Malus.

"Men and women of The Enlightened," his voice boomed across the field of soldiers. "Today, we stand on a precipice. We look into the abyss and hold fast against its seductive pull. On this day, we strike out to the heart of our enemy. No longer will we fight from the shadows for what we believe in. We shall announce to the world that The Enlightened and our holy charge is righteous and just. Too long has this world reveled in decadence. It is with a heavy heart that we heed the call of the Founder. The culling is nigh, and we must complete the cycle. Those who rebelled will not stand against the tide. We are that tide. We will wash away this trampled and sickened world and it will be born anew in the light. Go, my brothers and sisters, begin the cleansing. Know that your actions in the battle to come will reverberate across space and time. All who come after us will know, that it was our people, our sacrifice, that brought peace and harmony to this earth. The Founder's will, be done."

Thousands of voices shouted in unison, "The Founder's will, be done!"

The projection faded and the battalion commanders took charge of their perspective groups. The soldiers moved with calculated precision off of the field. In the next day, they would travel to their designated target and destroy their enemies. The resolve was absolute, and would not be swayed.

The console that stood in front of Primus and Simon came to life. It was Malus's voice that came from the speakers.

"Praetor," Malus said. His voice was smooth and calm. A somewhat jarring shift from the commanding and inspiring voice they all listened to only moments ago.

"Lord Malus," Primus said, as he performed a perfunctory bow.

"Our agents embedded in the government have ensured that the area around Lemuria will be evacuated. We don't need any witnesses. The Earthborn believe that the volcano is in danger of erupting."

"Very good, Lord," Primus said. His face was a mask devoid of emotion.

"My contact in the Collective will begin Phase Two of our plan," Malus said silkily.

"Lord, as your Praetor, should I not be privy to all aspects of our battle plan? What is Phase Two?"

Malus's deep voice chuckled. "Concentrate on the frontal assault, Praetor. Leave the rest to me."

"Yes... Lord," Primus said.

"Simon," Malus called.

"Yes, my lord?"

"I believe the experiments were successful. Take your place and power up the weapon. You will have a front row seat at the destruction of our enemies."

"Yes, Lord Malus. Thank you," Simon said quietly.

"You sound unenthusiastic," Malus said, judgment oozing from the speaker.

"No... my lord. No, it's just that the Tablets draw a lot of energy from me. They've been affecting me in a strange way, my lord. I'm simply tired. I will be prepared for our attack, I assure you."

"The Tablets are ancient. Their inner workings are still somewhat of a mystery and any knowledge of them has all but faded away from memory. Take heart. Yours is a blessed task. You will be successful. Victory or death."

"Victory or death," Simon echoed, his voice shallow and haunted.

The console powered down. Primus looked at Simon with concern. "I will come with you to the control station, Simon. We all have to stay on task if our plans are to be successful."

CHAPTER TWENTY-FIVE

CALM BEFORE THE STORM

Alana looked over at Max, who was sitting with his parents talking animatedly. Plato was with them, as well, but he seemed to keep his distance, as if he didn't want to impose on the Hunters' family time.

Strange, Alana thought.

They were all in the apartment in the middle of Lemurian City. War Preparations had been made and everyone had their assignments. They were as ready as they were going to be. The day before, intel came into headquarters that the host of The Fallen force had been deployed. Moving that many troops under cover and concealment was a slow process, but with the technology available to the Atlantean people that process was considerably faster than usual. Now, all they had to do was wait. Like so many soldiers had done through the millennia, Alana and their circle of friends spent time with their families before the battle. Except, Alana didn't really have any family. Her only family was her brother. Her enemy. It broke her heart to think about it. She had gone through most of her life thinking she was an orphan. Growing up, her only semblance of family was Plato. Then, her brother came blazing back into her life, but as a foe. She still had trouble coming to terms with those facts. Osiris, of course, was in a very similar boat. She could have taken solace with him, after all, misery loves company. But, Osiris was a lone wolf.

At least he likes to think he is, Alana mused.

He was the moody and distant brother Alana never really had.

Alana smiled. She amended her thoughts slightly. She did have family. Alana's family, what she considered to be family, was all in that room. Plato, Charlotte, Ronin, Wayland, Auggie, Osiris, and even Ayako. Ayako, in the past week, had grown on her. They bonded very quickly as they planned the battle strategies together. She was a kindred spirit.

She looked over at Max again. She didn't know how to feel towards Max. He was a close friend and confidant. But, he was also... more. Alana felt protective of him. Ever since he came into her life, she could no longer envision her life without him in it in some fashion. Max was definitely... more.

Lara looked up and caught Alana's eye. She smiled warmly and beckoned her over to join them at the dinner table. They had all finished supper some time ago, but the Hunter family, including Plato, all sat continuing to sip coffee and talk. Alana grabbed a mug of coffee and sat down with them. She instinctively sat by Max, a fact that Lara did not fail to notice. Lara smiled inwardly.

"Alana," Lara said warmly, "Max tells us that you've been his guardian angel since the day we were attacked and, subsequently, kidnapped."

Alana glanced at Max, who was smiling proudly.

She grinned. "He seems bound and determined to get himself in every possible dangerous situation."

"Well, not much has changed then," Jack said cheerfully. "Max has been getting himself into sticky situations since he was a baby. I mean, literally. Remember the incident with the honey?" Jack laughed.

Lara laughed as well. She was mid-way through taking a sip of coffee when she spluttered slightly back into the cup. "Oh, my goodness, yes!" She turned to Alana. "Max was nine or ten and I was studying ancient Egyptian healing practices, specifically their use of honey on wounds. Jack and I were talking about how honey could be used for several medicinal purposes over dinner. Max was sitting there listening to us and halfway through dinner…"

"Mom, come on," Max said, as he blushed.

Lara continued as she brushed Max's protest aside. "Halfway through dinner he gets up, leaves the dining table, and goes to the kitchen. He's gone for ten minutes or so. Jack and I noticed that Max had been gone for quite some time. We go into the kitchen and there is Max. Sitting on the floor, covered in honey!" Lara burst into laughter.

"The kid looked like he took a bath in the stuff," Jack added, also laughing heartily.

Their merriment was infectious. Plato and Alana laughed as well, but Max just shook his head grinning.

"I got a cut on my knee earlier that day at recess," Max tried to explain. "I thought the honey could help me."

"But why…" Alana guffawed. "Why did you pour it all over yourself?"

"Honey tastes good," Max explained simply. "After I poured some on my cut, I tried to pour some in my mouth. The lid came loose and boom. Honey shower."

The group laughed again. "Like I said," Jack exclaimed. "Sticky situations. That's why we are so thankful for you, Alana."

Alana smiled and looked down at her hands. "It's nothing, really. We look out for each other."

"Max is our only son," Jack said, looking Alana in the eyes. "To the Atlantean world, Max is the Key. He represents a chance for balance, a chance for our people to find purpose once again. But, to us…" Jack glanced at Lara, "…he's our son. Our flesh and blood. A parent's love for their child is forever and if anything were to happen to him, our world would be shattered."

Lara sniffed and wiped her eyes.

"So," Jack continued, "when we say we are so thankful for you, Alana, know that you have helped secure the most precious thing in the world to my wife and I. We will forever be in your debt."

Alana didn't know what to say. She continued to stare at her hands. Then, she felt a warm hand on her shoulder. Lara was staring intently at her. "You are part of *our* family now," she said softly. "You will always have our gratitude and love."

Alana's eyes welled up and her vision blurred. Plato, who was sitting across from her, reached across the table and put his hand on hers. His hand was warm and seemed to radiate affection.

"Thank you," Alana said, as she sniffed.

The doorbell rang. Everyone in the flat looked up.

"Wrench is at the door," Auggie said.

Wayland, who was playing cards with his parents on the carpet, jumped up to answer it. "No cheating, dad." Wayland's father shook

178

his head emphatically. Wayland opened the door and Wrench craned his neck to look up at Wayland.

"Man, you're big," Wrench said in awe.

"Uh... thanks, I think," Wayland said. "Come on in."

Plato saw Wrench walk in and he stood. "Master Wrench. To what do we owe the pleasure?"

"Actually, here to talk to Elders Lara and Jack," Wrench said, still staring at Wayland.

"Dude, stop," Wayland said frowning. "It's weird when you stare."

Wrench shook his head. "Right. Sorry. Be cool, Wrench."

"Wrench," Jack called. "Join us."

Wrench sat giddy as a schoolboy. "Hi guys!"

"Hey, Wrench," Max said, as he smiled. "What's up?"

"Well," he said, as he looked at Lara and Jack. "I think we're done! Lady Sotera and I have been working off of the designs you came up with and I think we got it all figured out!"

"Really?" Lara asked excitedly. "We should go and run tests," she said to Jack.

"Absolutely," Jack agreed.

"What's ready?" Max asked.

"The Titan," Jack smiled.

Max knew that smile. It was the same smile his dad got whenever he was on the verge of making a new discovery in archaeology. Or, when he was talking about his latest favorite book.

"We were briefed about it, but I'm afraid the information was rather limited," Alana said.

179

"That's because we didn't know much at the time," Plato said. "Honestly, we still don't know much."

"Where did that thing even come from?" Wayland asked.

"Indeed," Charlotte said from the other side of the room. "My mother and I had no knowledge of the Titan and it was sitting hidden in our own kingdom, for who knows how long."

Max looked around the room and realized that everyone had stopped what they were doing to listen to their conversation.

"Well, I have some idea," Plato said, as he rubbed his chin. "It was during the Fall; right before the destruction of Posidea, the capital city of the Empire of Atlantis, many thousands of years ago. The Leviathan had just been constructed. Malus was threatening to use it. Everyone was scrambling to find a way to combat it. Even the Key, Venator, was desperately trying to find a way to destroy the accursed machine. We searched the Hall of Records, we combed through the Shi'tal Codex, frantically hoping to find some bit of ancient knowledge that would help fight the destructive power the Leviathan represented. Those in the Order of Light had shunned Wayland the Smith at that point, but he was repentant. He realized that his hubris had doomed our people to destruction. In his guilt, he worked in secret to build something to counter the Leviathan. Although he was a brilliant engineer and inventor, it was Da Vinci's design mastery that made the Leviathan so formidable. In Wayland's final months, he created the Titans - Four massive automatons with specialized capabilities. Each one alone was no match for the Leviathan, but together, the Titans would, in theory, be worthy opponents. Wayland went to Venator and asked for forgiveness and his help. Venator saw what Wayland was trying to accomplish and he decided to help. Venator leant his power to the Titans, giving them an unlimited supply of energy."

"He could do that?" Max asked quietly.

"You'd be surprised at what you will be capable of one day, Max," Plato said. "But, even Venator's power was not enough. Malus caught wind of the construction of the Titans and he attacked this mountain before the Titans could be completed."

"Here?" Osiris asked from the kitchen. "Why were the Titans here?"

"Well, before this mountain was host to the Sacred Realm of Lemuria, it was Wayland the Smith's workshop," Plato said.

"The whole thing?" Wayland said astonished. "The whole mountain was his workshop?"

"Yes," Plato answered. "He cleared out this mountain and learned to control the volcanic instability. He made the most wondrous things here. When Malus attacked, he destroyed three of the four Titans. It was also, unfortunately, when Wayland the Smith met his end."

"So, this last Titan," Max said, "why wasn't it destroyed?"

"Each Titan was specialized," Plato answered. "They were specifically built to harness the four elements of the planet - Earth, water, wind, and fire. In the last few days, we have recovered Wayland's logs and schematics of the Titan Project. From what we can gather, the last Titan, the Titan of fire, was under construction deep within the mountain, utilizing the magma of the volcano for power. Malus never knew it was down there. After the three Titans were destroyed, stories of their very existence passed into legend. The Titan project was forgotten."

"The Titan Project is thousands of years old. How is an ancient old hunk of junk supposed to go up against the Leviathan?" Wayland asked.

"It depends on who pilots the hunk of junk," Lara replied coolly.

"Which I still don't agree with, Lara," Plato said.

"Dad, we don't have Venator to power this thing or Wayland the Smith to finish building it. Our retrofit and redesign is the only way we can get that metal monster to work, which means we have to use pilots to run it. Wayland the Smith never finished installing the automation components. We were lucky to finish the upgrades we thought up in the first place. Jack and I helped design it. We are the best qualified to pilot it."

"Wait, what?" Max exclaimed.

"Max," Jack said soothingly. "The Fallen are sure to use to the Leviathan. We all know that. The Titan is our best bet to fight it."

"Dad, didn't you hear Plato's story? Wayland the Smith designed these robots to fight together as a team - Four of them to take out one Leviathan. One Titan isn't going to hold up against it," Max said, a little hysterically.

"We won't be alone," Jack countered. We have dropships fitted with weapons that provide air support. All we have to do is hold off the Leviathan, keep it busy, until our ground forces can defeat The Fallen army. Once we win the ground battle, our forces will redeploy and attack the Leviathan with our full might. Ten thousand years ago, they didn't have the weapons that we have today. This is the best plan."

Max looked over at Ayako, who nodded solemnly.

"I don't..." Max was at a loss for words.

"The Titan is powerful," Lara said. "This *will* work."

Max nodded ruefully. He looked to Alana, but her eyes did not convey the comfort that he was hoping for. Instead, her eyes reflected his, full of only doubt and worry.

CHAPTER TWENTY-SIX

BLOOD THICKER THAN WATER

Ayako and Wrench stood in front of a flight of Spartans. The night prior had been a late one. Everyone in the group was groggy and sleepy. They had all stayed up swapping stories and listening to Plato talk about 'the ancient times'.

"I know everyone is tired," Ayako said, but you guys need to listen to Wrench. Piloting these things is not easy."

"Sorry, love," Osiris yawned. "Wrench can't put together two sentences to save his life. No offense, mate. How are we supposed to pay attention to him?"

"At any rate, Ayako-san," Ronin said, as he stifled his own yawn. We won't be in these confounded machines any way. We are all going to be assisting with the frontal assault.

"If you know your enemy, and you know yourself, you will not be afraid of the outcome of any battle," Ayako said. Her eyes were closed, as if she was recalling an old lesson. "Part of knowing yourself, is knowing the tools that you will be fighting with. At some point, you might have to pilot one of these. Besides the dropships, these Spartans are our only air defense."

"Plato is just trying to keep us all busy," Osiris scoffed. "He doesn't want us getting all antsy, now does he?"

"I'm sure he wants to avoid any of his people getting into fights with locals, as some of us tend to do when we're antsy," Alana smirked.

"How many times do I have to say it? That crazy fanatic picked a fight with me. Max, back me up," Osiris said with his hands on his hips.

Max looked between Alana and Osiris several times. "So, Wrench, how do we control the cannons again?"

"Figures," Osiris said. "Can't go against your sweetheart, can you? Bah! You lot stay and learn about these flying tin cans. I've scored perfectly on the simulator already. I'm going to fetch me a nap."

Osiris began to walk away when Max called after him. "Oz, wait up." Max ran to him and slowed to walk by his side. "Hey, how you doin'?"

"I'm fine. Just a little tired. We were up…"

"No, I mean, how are you doing, you know… with… your dad?"

Osiris stopped and stared at Max, as anger flashed in his eyes.

"We haven't had time to talk since we found out about your dad," Max said tentatively. "Now, we are about to go up against him. That has to be hard. I just want to make sure you're ok," he finished.

"You want to make sure I'm not going to turn on you, right?" Osiris' voice was full of venom.

"What?! No! That's not it at all," Max said surprised. "No one questions your loyalty, Oz. I just…"

"So, what is it then?" Osiris said angrily. "You want to know if I can fight my own dad? You want to know if I can kill him? I don't know, alright?! I don't know, Max."

185

The rest of the group was only a few yards away. They all turned to see what was going on.

"I'm not saying that either," Max bellowed. "I just want to see if you're ok. You're my friend. I worry about my friends. When a friend finds out that his dad has switched sides, I figure that might mess with their head a little."

Osiris shoved Max hard in the chest. Max stumbled back a few feet.

"Max," Wayland called.

Max held up a hand. "I'm fine."

Osiris was breathing heavily, his eyes were welling up. "I don't believe it, Max. Not for one second. My dad is not a traitor. He was a complete ass. Growing up, he always pushed me too hard. He never thought I was as good as I needed to be. I could never measure up in his eyes. All in all, he was a terrible father." Osiris wiped his eyes with the back of his hand. "But... he is *not* a traitor!"

Max's own anger instantly faded. He held his hands out to the side. "Ok, Oz. Ok. I'm with you. We're friends and if that is what you truly believe, then I got your back. But, we have to plan for the worst. What if he shows up? Then what?"

Osiris's shoulders sagged. "I don't... I don't know," he whispered.

Alana walked past Max and put her hand on Osiris's shoulder. "If that happens, we will deal with the problem like we've dealt with all our problems," she said soothingly. She looked back at Max. "Together."

BOOM!

CHAPTER TWENTY-SEVEN

ATTACK ON LEMURIA

The ground shook and the group instinctively dropped to one knee. All around, sirens blared to life. Residents of Lemuria began to scream and run in panic.

"What's happening?" Wayland yelled.

BOOM!

Ayako was on her tablet and rapidly called up the camera feeds across the city. "It looks like a couple of small explosions on the far side of the city."

Max looked across the metropolis and, from their elevated vantage point at the airstrip, he could see a curl of smoke rising into the air.

Charlotte gasped and turned to Ronin, "Ronin, it's the palace!"

Ronin took off running with Charlotte close on his heels. They each jumped into a Spartan and blasted into the sky. Max looked at Alana and she waved them on. "Come on, follow them!" The rest of the group climbed into a Spartan.

As soon as Max sat down, he could feel the neural connectors latch onto his suit. Max gasped, as the suit's operating system came online. The surge of power from the suit's reactors made Max's skin tingle slightly. Max grabbed the joysticks with each hand and, as he did, the automated H.U.D. came into view over the cockpit's canopy. Max pressed down with his toes on the pedals and the Spartan's boosters fired up. Max was jettisoned into the sky. The power of the Spartan was definitely impressive. He angled the vehicle towards the ever-increasing cloud of smoke.

Max saw the icons of his friends in his display; their names were attached to each square icon. They flew at his side, like birds of prey, as they swooped low over the cityscape. Below them, the city was in turmoil. Security personnel tried to rally everyone at designated checkpoints, but Max knew all too well that when people panic all logic goes out the window.

In the distance, Max saw the small icons of Ronin and Charlotte, as they descended to the ground at the palace. Within seconds, Max and the rest of the group also set their Spartans down. They all climbed out and the onslaught of smoke, fire, and screams hit them like a wall. Emergency workers were just arriving. Firefighters went to work, putting out the flames, while more security personnel did their best to control the crowds.

Ronin and Charlotte ran towards the palace gates and the rest of the group followed. As he ran, Max took a moment to assess the damage. As far as he cold tell, the only things on fire were the two hover cars that were parked in front of the palace.

"Did someone try to car bomb the palace?" Max yelled.

"I don't know," Alana said, over her shoulder. "It doesn't look like the cars tried to drive into the castle walls. They're just parked. Auggie, tap into the security feeds around the palace. Look for any footage of this area before the explosions happened."

"Compliance," Auggie said. "Search complete. The cars were unoccupied when they exploded. Nor were there any people in the vicinity of the blast when they occurred."

"That makes no sense," Ayako said. "Why set off bombs if you're not trying to hurt…"

Ayako stopped running. Max, Alana, Wayland, Osiris, and Auggie stopped as well. "We… need to get to the command center," Ayako said urgently, and she ran off towards the palace again.

"What the crap?" Wayland said, as they all ran after her.

The guards at the palace gates moved aside when they saw the group running in. They ran through the Great Hall and through the doors that lead down a hallway to the makeshift command center. Ronin and Charlotte were there already with Alastriona and Plato.

"It's a distraction," Ayako yelled, as she burst through the doors.

Plato looked up. "From what?" he asked.

Ayako climbed on the round table in the center of the room.

"Ayako, that table is very old," Alastriona admonished.

Ayako set her tablet at her feet then pressed a button on it. Form the four corners of the room, micro-digital projectors flared on. The room's walls were covered in a projection of the outdoors.

"I've set up this room to be a battlefield command center," Ayako said, as she slipped on a pair of black metallic gloves. "These haptic gloves allow us to zoom in on the 360 degree feed of the battlefield." She brought her hands together and then pulled them apart slightly. The camera zoomed in to a patch of land. "What we are looking at is the front entrance of Lemuria."

Max walked forward. His mind was having trouble accepting what he was seeing. It was as if he were outside, in the snow, on Mt. Rainer. His leg bumped into a chair, shattering the illusion.

"If this is a feed of our front entrance, then all is clear," Osiris said looking.

"Except, it's not," Ayako said, as she grabbed her tablet. Her fingers danced on the screen, punching in complicated codes. The micro-projectors went dark for a split second. When they came back to life, they were standing in the same location, but instead of an open field, Fallen soldiers surrounded them. Wayland jumped back from a soldier who seemed to be standing right next to him.

"What is this?" Ronin asked aghast.

Ayako put her tablet down then twisted her hands together. The view of the field changed. They were now looking at the field from a top down view. The open area in front the mountain was covered with Fallen troops. Tanks and sonic cannons were poised on the outskirts of the main force. Dropships bristling with pulse cannons hovered ominously over the throngs of soldiers. Thousands covered the field.

"Someone tampered with our feed," Alana said bemused. "Someone from the inside. They were able to sneak right up on us."

"Yep. Probably the same person who set off the car bombs," Ayako confirmed. "Now, they have the upper hand. They are setting the tempo of this dance."

"Plato, what now?" Alastriona asked horrified.

Plato looked to Ayako. "It seems our previous plan might not be valid, I'm afraid. What do you think, Ayako-san? Frontal attack?"

She nodded a couple of times while she stared off into space. Her gaze snapped back into focus. She made a motion with her hands and the view of the landscape changed once again to reveal an image of the Titan. "Okay. New plan."

CHAPTER TWENTY-EIGHT

BEACON NEWS

"Good morning, everyone. For those of you just tuning in, we are covering what seems to be a military operation on the outskirts of Mt. Rainer. Only hours ago, military aircraft was seen landing in the vicinity of Mt. Rainer, located 54-miles southeast of Seattle, Washington. Mt. Rainer is an active stratovolcano, but a major eruption has not occurred since 1894. Military operations on U.S. soil are no small thing. It speaks to the magnitude of this situation. Officials have quarantined a 20-mile radius around the mountain, to include the airspace, for safety of the public. Speculations are abound, but an inside source claims that the area is a secret operating location for the terrorist group that has caused much of the recent wanton destruction around the world. As mentioned earlier, these recent attacks have been coined as The History Bombings. A specific terrorist group has yet to claim responsibility for these bombings, but authorities have linked the separate attacks as one coordinated effort. We are not sure of the size of the force that is being utilized to oust the criminals from their hideout, but we have reason to believe that the terrorists are heavily armed and willing to deploy a large assortment of weapons. Our correspondent, Megan Crusher, is on scene to cover the events as they unfold. Megan?"

"Thank you, Linda. Yes, it is very hard to see, but in the far distance behind me there is a military force of some sort assembling in the open valley on the west side of Mt. Rainer. This is a fairly unpopulated area, but officials have said that the evacuation of civilians has already occurred. Citizens of Seattle and all surrounding cities have been placed on high alert. We are not sure where their target might be, but for the past hour, we haven't seen much activity from the force on the ground. Inclement weather has also been a factor here, as you can see, but we are staying vigilant, as this situation will surely escalate. For now, back to you, Linda."

"Thank you, Megan, and stay safe. Please stay tuned as our continuing coverage of the *Mt. Rainer Stand Off* unfolds."

CHAPTER TWENTY-NINE

TO WAR

Ayako's hands were a blur, as she manipulated the virtual map. All around the war room, the images constantly shifted. Everyone was experiencing a little bit of vertigo, but Ayako seemed unaffected. Max noticed that Ayako was placing markers at different intervals across the battlefield. An ominous glowing red X represented each marker.

"Elder Plato is right," Ayako said, as she continued her work. "We don't have time to execute our old plan. The whole thing was contingent upon early detection. Since our sensors were hacked and tampered with, we no longer have that luxury. Now, I have a dozen pilotless Spartan's sitting in the woods," she spat angrily. "We are going to have to resort to a full frontal attack. Ronin?"

"Yes, Ayako-san?"

"You rally the battalions. Have the Four Horsemen march their troops out at the front entrance. Then, stand fast. Wait for my signal to attack."

"Won't we be vulnerable to attack?" Ronin asked.

"Use the Casters that are embedded in each battalion. If need be, they can provide coverage with their abilities."

"I have got to meet these Caster people," Max said quietly to Alana.

"As you say, it will be done," Ronin said to Ayako.

"We have the element of surprise still," Ayako said, calling up an image of the Spartan mechs. "The Fallen do not know we have these things and they are extremely effective and brilliantly designed."

"Oh, stop it," Wrench said embarrassedly.

Alana ignored him and plowed on. "I need Osiris, Charlotte, Alana, and Max to take the Spartans we have here at the palace and fly out over the enemy and do strafing runs. They won't be able to react fast enough when you guys fly out, but you have to fly hard and fast. This is how we can get in a sucker punch to distract them. Coordinate your attack with Ronin. That way, The Fallen will be too busy taking cover from the airstrike and they won't bother with Ronin's forces forming up."

Alana nodded. "Done."

"Elder Plato, I need you to gather what remaining pilots we have and somehow sneak them out into the forest so they can get to the Spartans that are already staged. If we can get the timing right, The Fallen will be fighting the battle on three different fronts. Divide and conquer."

"I think I can manage it. The forest to the east will provide sufficient cover. I will oversee their movement myself," Plato said nodding.

"Wayland. Auggie. Take the last two Spartans and go to the rear entrance. Auggie, gather the Primordials and prepare them to fight. It doesn't look like there is any enemy movement on that side of the mountain, but we need to play it safe. If you get overwhelmed, I'll know and I'll send reinforcements."

Auggie morphed into a soldier and saluted smartly. "Yes, ma'am!"

"Wrench, go to Lady Sotera and help her with maintenance on the flight line. We have to launch our dropships in the next 15 minutes. That means, they have to be fully flight ready in the next 10. They will be the only other air support we have until we can get the pilots to their Spartans."

"On my way," Wrench said, as he left the room.

"What should we do?" Jack asked.

"You and Elder Lara *are* the frontal attack," Ayako said. She pulled the interior of the mountain up on the holo-display. "You will launch the Titan from its platform through the top of the mountain. I'll deactivate the laser grid as you pass then reactivate it once you're clear. By the time you land here," she said as she pointed to a marker on the map of the battlefield, "the strafing runs will have taken their toll on The Fallen forces. The Titan will decimate most of the enemy. Once that happens, Ronin will lead his battalions forward and engage. The Spartans in the woods will have their pilots by then, so we should have the upper hand. Victory will be ensured."

"What about the Leviathan?" Max said.

"We haven't received any reports that it is present," Ayako said. For the first time that morning, she looked worried. "If it does show up, then... well, I guess we'll cross that bridge when we get there. That's all I have, I think. Queen Alastriona and I will remain here to oversee that non-combatant personnel get to shelter in the great library and we'll be here in the war room where we will coordinate the battle.

We will have eyes on all of you, I promise. If you get into trouble, know that we'll be doing everything we can to get you help," Ayako said.

The group nodded. They knew Ayako was capable of leading their army; they trusted her with their lives. "Everyone," Plato said, as he looked each one of them in the eye in turn. "Be safe, take care of each other. We are stronger together than we are apart," he said, as he looked poignantly at Alana. "Go. May the Founder watch over us all."

Max began to follow Alana out of the war room. Jack caught his arm. "Max," he said urgently. Max turned and saw his mom and dad standing there. "Fight hard, Son. Stay safe."

"We love you, Maxy," Lara said, as she hugged Max hard.

"I love you both," Max said. He began to walk off then turned quickly. "I'll see you after this is all done."

Jack nodded and squeezed Lara to his side and they watched their son leave to fight this war.

* * *

Max climbed the built-in ladder on one of the Spartan's legs. Throughout Lemuria, alarms blared, but the people seemed to be less panicked and more focused. They walked quickly towards the palace to take shelter in the library deep underground. The citizens who chose to fight ran towards the staging area where the Warrior Guild battalions were formed up. Max saw Ronin in that same direction. Wayland passed below and called up to Max.

"Be safe, brother," Wayland yelled.

Max looked down and smiled. "Yeah, you too, Way. Remember, always be…"

"Always be afraid," Wayland said. "Yeah, yeah."

With Auggie by his side, Wayland walked off towards his own Spartan.

"Watch out for him, Aug," Max said quietly to himself as he watched them go. To Max's surprise, Auggie's head turned a full 180 degrees and he gave Max a thumbs up. Max smiled and waved one last time before he descended into the cockpit of his war machine.

The neural links clacked into place as Max sat down. His Spartan's console came to life and he gripped the joysticks of the mech.

"Systems check," Alana said over their comm-link.

"Check," Osiris and Charlotte said, almost in unison.

Max checked a readout on his console and saw all green lights next to his mech's systems report. "Check," he finally said.

"Copy," Alana said. "Ronin, do you read?"

"Loud and clear, Alana," Ronin said.

"We are ready to launch," she said. "Give us the word and we'll rain fire on The Fallen."

"Outstanding," Ronin said enthusiastically. He was breathing hard, but his voice was layered in anticipation and excitement.

"Someone's ready to rock and roll," Osiris said, laughing slightly.

"Yes. Yes, I am," Ronin responded. "Stand by. I am going to address the troops."

Alana left the channel open so they could listen. She thought for a moment and then pressed a button to broadcast Ronin's feed to all friendly forces' comm-links. Now, the whole of the Lemurian force was tuned in to Ronin.

"Brothers, sisters, our time has come! The Fallen, like a snake in the grass, have crept up and are ready to strike. They come to destroy our way of life and our people. Defend our home, but most of all, on the field of battle, defend one another. We have all faced hardship and sacrifice. We know what it means to lose those whom we've loved. It is for this very reason that we stand here united against the darkness. That darkness wishes to take from us all that we hold dear. But, we will not let it. We will not falter. We stand strong together! Let us give onto these scoundrels the gift of battle. The bards will sing of our deeds for ages to come, and our legacy will live on through eternity. To war!"

CHAPTER THIRTY

LAUNCH

Max pressed down on the acceleration pedals in the Spartan. Its rockets fired on his back and the massive mech lifted off of the ground.

"Turn on your guidance system," Alana said over the comm. "There are only a few lava tubes that actually lead to the outside. The guidance software will tell us where to go."

"Let's do this," Osiris said. "I have to admit, Ronin got me fired up!"

"He is a natural leader," Charlotte said fondly.

"Let's go and give your fiancé some air cover," Osiris said. "Loser has to buy dinner!" Osiris rocketed away.

Forgetting he was about to fight an entire army, Max felt giddy with playful excitement. He gunned his accelerator and his mech shot off like a bullet.

"Boys," Alana sighed, as she followed after them. "Let's go, Charlie."

"Right behind you," she said, as she laughed.

The four of them flew to one of the walls that made up the perimeter of the city. Max followed his guidance system as it superimposed a flight path on his heads-up display. The Spartan was very responsive, but the controls were also forgiving. Wrench designed the Spartans so they could be easily piloted by anyone with minimal training.

They found the lava tunnel they were looking for. The opening to the tube was massive. Their Spartans flew through without any problems.

"These tubes can be a bit tricky," Charlotte said. "There are numerous twists and turns. I suggest auto-pilot until we clear the tunnel."

"No way," Osiris said. "This is way too much fun!" As soon as the words left his mouth, his Spartan's shoulder bashed into the side of the rock tunnel. A shower of sparks flew back and blinded Max for a split. "Right," Osiris said, as he cleared his throat. "Auto-pilot it is."

After a few minutes, they emerged from the tunnel. Snow and rocks trailed behind them as they punched through the partially closed-off opening.

"Stay low," Alana warned. "We don't want to give away our position."

Max landed his Spartan next to Osiris on an outcropping on the side of the mountain. He magnified the optics on his mech and saw The Fallen force. The number of soldiers and vehicles was astounding.

"We're supposed to fight that?" Max said apprehensively.

"Unfortunately," Osiris answered.

"Ronin, Ayako, we are in place," Alana said.

"Stand-by," Ayako said. "Ronin, we will move on your command."

At the base of the mountain, Ronin stood just inside of the secret entrance of Lemuria. Behind him, four separate battle groups waited anxiously. Ronin smiled back at the Four Horsemen. "Are you ready, brothers?"

The all nodded gravely.

"Ready," Ronin called over the comm-link. His voice was steely and calm.

Alana launched her Spartan from the precipice of the mountain. Max, Osiris, and Charlotte followed. They maneuvered their mechs over the surface of the mountain until they were heading due west. In front of them, the sprawling mass of Fallen soldiers came within range.

"Weapons free," Alana said. "Spread out, you don't want them to be able to lock on to you."

Max angled his Spartan down. We switched the mech into an air-to-ground configuration. The legs of the mech bent forward, giving it better hover capabilities. Max simultaneously pushed the acceleration to its peak and fired the sonic cannons that were mounted on the Spartan's arms. Hundreds of soldiers fell to the ground, clutching their ears in pain. Osiris dropped dozens of concussive bombs in concentrated areas of soldiers and the subsequent explosions instantaneously knocked out troops in a 20-foot radius of the point of impact. Alana targeted the remotely piloted aircraft in the air before they could open fire on them. Her plasma cannons fired and the superheated beams cut the metal hulls of the aircraft, causing them to burst in spectacular fashion. Charlotte took a more direct approach, flying low to the ground, firing her sonic cannons. In her wake, she left a swath of downed soldiers.

They completed their first strafing round and as they circled back, Max saw the mass confusion their attack caused. The soldiers who weren't hit stepped over their fallen comrades and trained their weapons on the Spartans. Several of the tanks in The Fallen arsenal rotated their turrets to track their attacker's flight path.

"Stay sharp. We poked the sleeping giant," Osiris said.

"Ronin, deploy," Ayako commanded over the comm.

At the entrance, Ronin and his comrades charged out, screaming their war cries. Max could see the Lemurian forces pour out of the mountain, like hundreds of angry army ants. "Watch your aim, guys," Max said. "Ronin and his forces are on the board."

"Roger," they all answered back.

The Spartan squad swooped low again to start their next bombing run. They began to take heavy fire from the tanks. Giant energy blasts zipped between Max and his friends. They all had to bank to avoid being hit. Max turned on his plasma cannons and set his weapons to rapid fire. He squeezed the trigger and his energy bolt hit home. Dozens of Fallen soldiers fell from his blasts. Max felt strange suddenly. He stopped firing and pulled back on his joysticks. The Spartan banked up sharply.

"Max, what are you doing?" Alana asked.

"I can feel them," Max said in a panic. "I can feel all of them."

Max pitched high into the clouds out of range from enemy fire.

"Max, what's going on?" Ayako said.

"I can't..." Max said, almost hyperventilating. "When they die, I can feel it."

"What?!" Ayako said urgently. "We need you back in the fight," Ayako said.

Max, listen to me, Alana pushed.

Alana, I feel when they die. Why am I feeling that? I shouldn't be able to feel that, he responded in a panic.

I don't know. But, we need you, Max. Our friends are fighting and they will die if we don't help them. We need you.

Alana, you don't know what it felt like. So much fear, so much pain.

Use sonic blasts. Concussive rounds. Get back in the fight. Alana's thoughts were urgent, almost commanding.

Max took deep breaths. "Okay," he said aloud. "Okay."

Max banked down and rejoined the group as they circled around for another pass.

"Everybody good?" Osiris asked.

"Yeah," Max said. "Good."

"Alright, heads up. We're sending out the Titan," Ayako said. "Jack? Lara?"

"Pre-flight check complete. Ready for launch," Lara said.

"You're a go for launch," Ayako responded.

"Launch in t-minus 5, 4, 3, 2... 1," Jack said over the comm.

The rumble of the rockets filled the comm-channel, which was replaced by static, and then... dead air.

CHAPTER THIRTY-ONE

GROUND BATTLE

The Titan blasted from the volcano, a fiery mass that filled the cloud-strewn sky with hues of red and orange.

"We have full burn," Jack's calm voice said over the radio.

"Roger, Titan, we are tracking you now," Ayako said quickly. "Wait…"

"Say again, actual," Lara asked. "Did you say wait?"

"No…" Ayako whispered. "Titan… Titan divert. I repeat. Divert! Coordinates have been transmitted."

"Coordinates received," Lara said. "Actual, please confirm. These coordinates lead to the middle of the ocean."

"Affirmative, Titan. Be advised, the Leviathan is 20-miles off the coast of Washington state. You are to intercept to avoid civilian casualties. It's going to make landfall at Gray's Harbor within the next 30-minutes if we don't stop it. That's a lot of Earthborn lives."

"Coordinates laid in," Jack said. "En route."

"Wait. Wait! That's a fire Titan, right?" Max asked. "How well is that thing going to do in the water?"

"We'll make due, Max," Lara said. "Get your head back in the fight."

"Pilots have reached their Spartans," Plato's voice crackled over the radio. "Launching now."

Max switched his radio to a private channel and contacted Alana. "Alana, I'm going to help my parents. They don't know how the Titan is going to react in the water. Hell, they don't know how that thing is going to react, period."

"Max…"

"The other Spartans are online. They will more than take my place here. If the Leviathan breaks through… my parents, everyone here, we'll all be dead."

Alana was silent for a moment. Then, she sped off to the west of the battle.

"Hey, where are you going?" Max asked alarmed.

"Well… come on. Let's go fight a giant sea monster."

Max throttled up and his Spartan chased after her. "Thank you, Alana."

* * *

"Where the bloody hell are those two going?" Osiris asked, as he fired on a pulse cannon.

"I do not know," Charlotte said. "Actual, we have a little problem."

"Yeah, I see," Ayako said, as she watched the two markers indicating Alana and Max leave the map area. "Alana, come in." She was met with only silence. "Max, do you read?"

"I don't think we're getting them back," Osiris said. "They flew in the direction of the Leviathan. I'm going to go help them."

"No, Oz. Stay put. We can't afford losing another Spartan." Ayako rubbed her eyes in frustration. "Do you guys think I just pull these strategic plans out of thin air?" She shook out her hands in an attempt to clear her head. "Fine. New, *new* plan," she sighed.

"Um... Ayako?" Wayland's voice wavered over the radio.

Ayako pulled up the video feed of the back entrance. "Yes, Wayland. Are you okay?"

"Are these good guys or bad guys?" Wayland asked shakily. He stood in a line with Auggie and two-dozen Primordial Sasquatch.

In the feed, Alana saw huge creatures lumber out of the forest, making a beeline for Wayland's position.

"Those are Cryptids," Auggie said. "More commonly known as trolls." Fallen soldiers accompanied them. "I believe they are bad."

"Will you guys be okay?" Ayako asked. "Do you need...?"

One of the Primordials that formed the protective line around the entrance to Lemuria jumped high into the air towards the closest approaching Cryptid. Her roar made Wayland cringe. It even gave Ayako goose bumps through the comm-link. The Sasquatch came down on top of the troll, smashing it into the ground. They twitched once, then stopped moving altogether. The Sasquatch roared a challenge to the other Cryptids, who were now backing away slowly."

"Uhhhh... no, I think we're good," Wayland said.

On the other side of the mountain, Ronin battled valiantly. He cut down soldier after soldier. But, as hard as he fought, the hordes of The Fallen seemed to keep coming. "Ayako, we need reinforcements."

"The Spartans are working their way towards you," she responded. "They are going to have to land soon and fight on the

207

ground. Our forces are too intertwined to use airstrikes. We run the risk of friendly fire."

"No, they will be overtaken," Ronin bellowed, as he parried a battle ax and kicked his enemy in the stomach. "Have them continue their fire on the back of The Fallen army. We'll keep pressing forward. We'll meet in the middle."

"Your force is taking too much damage," Ayako said, as she watched the lights of friendly forces blink out sporadically across the map.

"Don't... the Spartans... best..." Ronin's comms went out.

"Ronin, come in," Ayako commanded. "Ronin."

"I'll find him," Charlotte said quickly.

"Charlotte, keep firing on the flanks. Stay air born. Ronin says it's too hot," Ayako said, panic creeping into her voice. "Do not land!"

"I see him!" Charlotte declared.

A cannon blasted, burning plasma towards Charlotte's Spartan, as she flew low towards Ronin. The plasma struck Charlotte's port engine. She rapidly lost altitude and her Spartan hurtled into the ground taking out several dozen Fallen in the process. Charlotte's indicator light winked out on the holo-display.

Alastriona bolted up at the table and searched the images in horror. She was powerless to stop the carnage.

CHAPTER THIRTY-TWO

THE SNAKE IN THE GRASS

Wrench worked feverishly on a pulse cannon. Drips of sweat fell from his head onto the barrel of the still hot weapon. He did his best to replace the motivator on the cannon so they could redeploy the weapon in the field, but the heat was almost unbearable. His elbow accidently touched the barrel, making Wrench jump back in pain.

"Ahh, stupid... hot... thing," Wrench said, as he nursed his burnt flesh.

"Give it here, laddy," Sotera said.

Wrench handed her the motivator. Sotera hefted the cannon with one hand. Her hand sizzled on the barrel, but she continued her work unperturbed. She placed the motivator in its compartment, then powered up the cannon. The weapon hummed to life. She turned it back off and placed it on the transport that was set to return back to the battlefield."

She glanced at Wrench, who was staring at her in awe. She held up her hand and it looked completely unharmed. "Ferrum Clan," she said proudly. "Fire is our friend."

"Awesome," Wrench said reverentially.

"Come, boy. We've got to get two more Phantoms airborne, not to mention about half a dozen..."

Wrench's comm-bracelet chimed. He frowned as he pressed the menu button. The display above his upturned palm showed a proximity alarm blaring. "That's weird."

"What's wrong?"

"One of the alarms at the geothermal reactor went off. It's gotta be a false alarm. No one is in that sector of the city," Wrench said, as he stared at his display.

"Well, go on, then. Check it out to be safe. Last thing we need is that reactor going boom. Hurry back though, we've a war to win."

"Yes, Lady Sotera," Wrench said obediently. He straddled a speeder that was parked close by and zipped away towards the reactor. The trip only took a few minutes.

Soon, Wrench was at the gates of his home and workplace. He walked through the security gates and noticed that they were bent out of shape.

"Okay. Don't freak out, Wrench. Don't freak out."

He proceeded into the facility and he was immediately on edge. Things in his workshop had been moved. To the casual visitor, Wrench's workshop looked like one big junkyard. What most people didn't know was that Wrench had an eidetic memory. He knew where every single nut and bolt was located.

"Someone touched my stuff," Wrench said to himself. "Ladies?" he called out. "Ladies, who touched my stuff?"

No answer.

Wrench began to panic. He moved from room to room looking for his robotic friends, but they were nowhere to be found. He descended down the stairs to the monitoring station, the place where the volcanic activity was regulated and controlled. There, in the middle of the room, were four automatons, battered and broken. "Nooo!" Wrench yelled. "Who did this?" he began to cry. "My friends... who did this to you?"

Wrench heard a noise behind him and he whirled around. His eyes went wide with surprise. "What are you doing...?"

*   *   *

Sotera looked in the corner of her vision. Her armor's neural link displayed the time. "Where did that boy get off to?" She called up her communications screen and called Wrench. The line rang several times before Wrench finally picked up. Sotera was startled by his appearance. He was leaned up against a console, blood dripping down his face. "What happened, lad? Where are you?"

"My... lady. He killed them. They were my best..."

"Wrench, I'm coming to get you, stay put." Sotera used her armor's software to locate Wrench. A GPS marker pinpointed his exact location.

"No. No time," he wheezed. "The generator... it's been tampered with. Rainer... is going to erupt. Judias. High Magus. It was him," Wrench grimaced in pain. "I can't stop it... I'm sorry. I'm sorry. Tell everyone... I'm sorry."

CHAPTER THIRTY-THREE

LOOK TO THE EAST

Osiris tracked Charlotte's descent. He knew that if he got close to the ground he'd probably take too much fire. The Horsemen and their clans were fighting like berserkers, but the supply of Fallen troops didn't seem to subside. A snowstorm was taking shape around them and visibility was steadily decreasing.

"Ayako, things are looking rather grim down here, love."

"I know. I'm watching the feeds. We are doing great, but The Fallen keep coming. Where are their reinforcements coming from?"

"I don't know," Osiris said, as he scanned the battlefield. "I saw where Charlotte crashed. I'm going down to help her."

"Oz," Ayako said seriously. "If you bring that Spartan within range, The Fallen will shoot you out of the sky. Please listen to me. Don't land that thing."

Osiris chuckled. "I would never disobey a direct order." Osiris linked the operating system of the Spartan with his M.A.R.S. armor, then he set the mech to hover on autopilot. He turned on the video feed in his cockpit and it connected to the war room. Ayako's face appeared on his display. "I'm not going to land, but I am going to help Charlotte and Ronin." He winked at Ayako, "Be right back, love." Osiris opened his cockpit, icy wind bit into his skin, and he jumped out of the Spartan.

Ayako watched in awe as Osiris free fell. She switched cameras to get a better angle of what was happening. One of the Lemurian pulse cannons happened to be pointing in Osiris's general direction, so she tapped into the video feed. Osiris punched through the cloud cover, his body straight as an arrow, hurtling toward the ground at terminal velocity.

Osiris did his best to calm his breathing. The cold wind rushed past his face, causing his eyes to tear up. He closed them, willing himself to calm down. He reached out with his mind and felt everything around him - the air, the clouds, the earth. Osiris tapped into his telekinesis and concentrated on his own body. With all his might, Osiris lifted his own body with his power. He had used this technique once before, but at the time, he was pushed off the edge of a cliff and it was his only option. Coincidently, it was extremely difficult for an Atlantean to lift their own bodies with telekinesis. One needed a base to push or pull from. You could push off the ground, but distance would soon win out and the efficacy of your power would wane. Osiris's solution was to pull at the Spartan as he fell, thus, slowing his descent. When he fell too far away from the Spartan, he would refocus his power and push up from the ground. In theory, it sounded simple. In reality, not so much.

Osiris was now closer to the ground than he was to the Spartan, so he refocused on pushing away from the ground. The wind around him subsided, but he was still falling at a good clip. Osiris pushed harder, mustering every once of power he had. He landed on two feet with a solid thud. His legs gave out somewhat and he dropped to one knee. "Ow, I hate that part."

"I've never seen anyone do that before," Ayako's voice rang.

"Yeah, well, I highly recommend against it. Killer on the knees." Osiris looked around and saw Charlotte's downed Spartan. "There's the mech. I'm going to go find the happy couple."

All around him, the fighting continued. Everywhere he looked, people were engaged in one-on-one combat. Osiris withdrew his swords and readied himself to fight. Osiris hopped on top of the Spartan to gain a better vantage point and what he saw made him smile from ear to ear. On the other side of the massive robot, Ronin and Charlotte stood in the middle of a large circle of Fallen warriors. The soldiers tried to surge forward, but each time they did, Charlotte or Ronin cut them down. Ronin laughed each time he swung his sword, clearly having the time of his life.

Osiris also noticed two other girls fighting beside Ronin and Charlotte. They weren't dressed like anyone in the Lemurian force or The Fallen army. One girl wielded two fighting knives and she had a bow and arrow strapped to her back. She spun like a tornado, dispatching three soldiers at once. Her technique was raw and powerful. The other, younger girl, stood in the middle of the three warriors, standing stalk still. Her arms were stretched outward and her hands glowed a strange blue light. Her eyes were closed and she looked like she was muttering something.

Osiris didn't have time to think about the oddity of these newcomers. He jumped down and began his attack. Osiris tried to move as quickly as he could. Taking out soldiers in one or two moves. He wanted to attack as efficient as possible, to maintain the element of surprise. Osiris soon carved a path to his friends. Ronin saw Osiris and smiled.

"Brother," Ronin yelled. "'Tis a glorious battle, is it not?!"

"Yeah," Osiris dodged a plasma bolt while simultaneously burying his sword into the soldier who fired at him. "It's grand. Who are your new," slash, "friends?" Snikt.

"Warriors from the Hunter Clan and the Caster Clan," Ronin said happily. "Sisters, no less."

"Cool," Osiris said, as he took a hit from a large war hammer on the shoulder. He grunted in pain, and then he ducked from another oncoming blow. "How have you guys stayed alive in this craziness for so long, if you don't mind me asking?" Osiris said casually, as he dispatched his attacker with a spinning heel hook.

"The Caster," Charlotte said, as she fired energy arrows from her bow, Victory. "She has placed a force barrier around us."

"What the bloody hell is a force barrier?" Osiris asked. He backed up and, as he did, his back touched the invisible barrier. It burned his back. "Ahhh! What is going on...?"

"Lilyana, let the new guy in," the girl with the knives called. Lilyana frowned, her concentration somewhat broken. "You're not always the one in charge, Jennavieve."

"Just do it," Jennavieve said annoyed.

An invisible force tugged at Osiris, yanking him into the protective circle. Ronin glance over to him and smiled, "Welcome."

Ayako was monitoring the audio feed Osiris's suit was transmitting when it suddenly shut off. "What the hell?" She tapped a command on her tablet, but nothing happened. "We just had him. His signal just shut off, like Ronin's and Charlotte's."

Sotera's face appeared in Ayako's holo-display. "Evacuate everyone! Now!" she yelled.

Ayako didn't hesitate. She pressed a button on her tablet. "Evacuation order alpha. I repeat, evacuation order alpha. All personnel proceed to any available exit route," she said into her tablet. Her voice was transmitted to all communication devices within the Collective. "It's done, Lady Sotera. What is going on?"

"The mountain is set to erupt. The geothermal reactor has been sabotaged by Judias. I don't know how much time we have, but you and the queen need to leave. I'm on my way to the reactor now. Wrench was hurt. Have to save the boy."

Ayako nodded. "We'll leave as soon as we can. Send me an update if you find anything new."

Sotera's feed disappeared. Ayako looked over at Alastriona. "I don't have contact with any of my combatant commanders.

Alana, Max, Osiris, any of them. I can't warn them about the eruption."

* * *

More soldiers surged forward. Osiris was beginning to feel weak. His energy levels were sapped.

"I can't hold this barrier much longer," Lilyana said, as beads of sweat formed on her face.

The ground shook and everyone in the immediate area paused. It shook again, this time more violently.

"What now?" Osiris said, exasperated.

In the distance, several large craft materialized in the air.

"Those are Goliath-class transports," Ronin said. "I didn't know they had cloaking technology on craft so large. There must be other ships in the area that are cloaked that are sending more Fallen troops into battle."

"What the hell do they need Goliath ships for? What are they hauling?" Osiris asked.

The bomb bay doors of the massive aircraft opened up and out dropped a house-sized cannon, ten times the size of normal plasma cannons. The ground shook again as the behemoth weapon landed on the field.

"Giant cannons. Great. I had to open my big mouth," Osiris said to himself.

"Those aren't normal cannons," Charlotte said. "I've seen those before. They're excavation cannons. Meant to punch holes through large structures."

"Like mountains," Ronin said in horror.

Osiris gripped his swords tighter. He was determined to fight until he couldn't fight anymore. The excavation cannons began to power up. Everyone, Fallen and Lemurian, stared up in hushed wonderment at the unprecedented display of power.

The air was suddenly punctuated with the piercing sound of a horn. The sonorous tone of the horn rang out across the battle torn valley. Osiris's attention was drawn to the east. The horn sounded again. There, on the ridge, emerged a long line of black clad warriors. At their center, a man wearing a long red headband stood with his sword raised high.

"Master Tzu!" Charlotte yelled. "Master Plato!"

Plato stood next to Tzu, a katana at his side.

"And, it looks like they brought every Iga ninja that Tzu has ever trained!" Osiris said whooping. The whole of The Fallen army turned to face the new threat. Tzu brought down his sword and his ninjas moved like a black wind - silent, swift, and ready to kill.

CHAPTER THIRTY-FOUR

BATTLE OF GODS

Max and Alana hovered next to the Titan off the coast of Washington state. Jack and Lara were able to find an elevated portion of the seabed to land on while they waited. The Titan stood in the water and the level came up to its waist. The mammoth mech was almost 200 feet tall, but the ocean in that region was deep.

"Do you see anything on the scanners?" Max asked.

"No," Lara said. "Max, you need to turn back. Let us handle this."

"I don't want to talk about it," Max said dismissively.

"Maxy, I will swat you right out of the sky, young man. Do not test me."

"Mom, I'm here, can we please just drop…"

From under the tumultuous surface of the ocean, the Leviathan suddenly rose. One hundred yards ahead of them, the mechanical beast stood to its full height. Max looked up. He had to angle his Spartan so he could see the head of the monster.

"At least 300 feet," Jack said in awe. "It is remarkable."

The Leviathan was serpentine in nature. Its curved body was encrusted with coral and other detritus from spending thousands of years at the bottom of the ocean floor. Underneath the earthly crust, shown a deep green metallic material. Max recognized its composition. It was the same metal the ancient Atlanteans used to build their great capital city of Posidea. It was the same metal that Wayland the Smith used to construct Max's nearly indestructible sword, Excalibur. Orichalcum.

"Big problem guys," Max said. "That thing is made of Atlantean metal. Really hard to penetrate."

"Oh, ye of little faith," Jack said. The Titan pulled from its back a large battle-ax. When the mech grasped the handle with both hands, the ax blazed to life. The blades of the ax bristled with hot blue fire and the shaft also glowed with the same flickering heat.

"What do you think our ax is made of?" Lara said proudly.

The Leviathan opened its maw, the reef that had formed on its jawline cracked from the sudden shift of the monster's jaw. A red ball of energy began to form in its mouth. It drew its head back and then violently jutted forward, like a snake striking out at its prey. The energy from the Leviathan's mouth shot forward. The Titan shifted in an attempt to dodge the beam, but it didn't move fast enough. The beam caught the metal knight on the shoulder and a large chunk of the armor plating blasted away.

Alarm claxons rang inside the cockpit of the Titan, but Jack and Lara maintained control. They moved the Titan forward, firing its thrusters. The Titan raised its battle-ax and swung the blade down. The water limited the Titan's ability to move. It was heavily plated and meant to withstand massive amounts of heat, but the water was clearly its nemesis. The Leviathan swerved to the side as the ax came down.

The snake-like creature raised its body even higher and came down on the Titan, its jaw ripping into the torso of the mighty robot.

Max and Alana flew up to the Leviathan's head and fired their plasma canons. They were like bothersome mosquitos in the shadow of the giant machine, but their aim struck directly in the joint section of the jaw. They focused their blasts at the exact same spot, doubling their power.

The Leviathan let go of the Titan and, as it pulled away, the Titan swung its ax again, only this time the blade of the ax found its mark. The fire imbued blade dug deep into the metallic hide of the serpent. The Titan placed its foot on the Leviathan so it could leverage its ax out.

Max and Alana continued their attack as well, coordinating their efforts, but having little effect. "Try targeting its optics," Alana said over the comm. "Maybe we can blind it," she said hopefully.

The Leviathan thrashed and its tail wrapped around the Titan. Max could hear the hull of the Titan creak and grown as the Leviathan constricted its tail. The Spartans flew up to the beast's head. The monster fired its red beam once more, but the Spartan mechs were agile machines. They split, going separate directions, dodging the concussive blast. They fired their cannons at one of the Leviathan's eyes, but the beams didn't seem to affect it.

"Getting a little tight down here," Jack said, as the Titan struggled to get free of the boa constrictor hold.

"Going to try something," Lara said. She flipped a switch and the entirety of the Titan burst into flames. The ocean water flash boiled around the mech as the heat intensified. "Don't think we can keep this up," Lara said, as she checked a gauge. This is eating through our energy supply really fast.

Out of frustration, Max began firing at anything he could target on the Leviathan. "We have to do something," he yelled.

Something large descended upon them from the sky. Max and Alana had to send their Spartans into a dive as a large creature with wings slammed into the head of the Leviathan. Max angled around and saw the golden form of Quetzalcoatl. The mechanical dragon that tried killing Max and his friends only months ago. The dragon ripped at the Leviathan's eyes, its claws leaving gaping rents in the metal body of the great sea monster. Max never believed he would be so happy to see that monster again.

The Leviathan loosened its grip on the Titan and Jack and Lara were able to rocket their way out. The full body burn sapped their power reserves preventing them from flying. They weren't able to sustain flight, so they dropped back down into the ocean.

"The dragon must be drawn to the power of the Tablets," Alana said. "It's still searching for them!"

The Leviathan whipped its head back and forth trying to dislodge the dragon from it's face. Max and Alana could only hover at a safe distance watching the battle play out, for what little good they could do.

Jack and Lara maneuvered the Titan around the back of the Leviathan and began hacking away at the monster's tail. With each stroke, they destroyed a piece of the beast. "We'll take this thing apart bit by bit," Jack said loudly.

The ocean around them began to heave as the storm took shape. Winds moved swiftly across the surface causing the water to spray in magnificent puffs of mist.

The Leviathan finally rid itself from the face-eating dragon with a powerful swish of its head. The golden dragon roared in defiance, as it flapped its powerful wings, hovering before the Leviathan. Then, in one deft motion, the Leviathan snapped forward, crushing its massive jaws around the would-be savior. Quetzalcoatl exploded in the mouth of the Leviathan, its mechanical parts sprayed across the water. The Leviathan turned its attention back to the Titan. Its eyes were now nothing more than two obliterated metal cavities, but its other sensors were very much still intact. The red energy blazed in its mouth anew.

CHAPTER THIRTY-FIVE

ERUPTION

The tide of the battle was finally turning in Lemuria's favor. Osiris fought with renewed vigor now that the Iga warriors were with them. After the force barrier went down, Ayako's map revealed the location of her lost combatant commanders.

"Not cool, you guys! Where have the three of you been?! I couldn't see anybody on my map," she said angrily.

"We're all good," Osiris said between blows. "Maybe that Caster girl's magic force barrier blocked out the reception or something. Craziest thing I've ever seen."

"That's all irrelevant," Ayako said promptly. "Pull all of our forces out, immediately."

"What?! Why? Ayako, your dad is here. He showed up with the Ninjas of Iga. I mean, like all of them. We're winning," Osiris said excitedly.

"My dad..." Ayako said quietly. She breathed a sigh of relief, but it was short lived. "Well, all of you need to get clear of the mountain. The queen and I are already on the move. I've sent Wayland, Auggie, and the Primodials away from here. I can't get ahold of Lady Sotera and Wrench. Osiris, it's going to erupt!"

As if on cue, The Fallen forces suddenly withdrew and ran back to their dropships and other various transports. The Lemurian forces were utterly bemused.

The blood drained from Osiris's face. "Ronin," he said quickly.

Ronin nodded, "Yes, I heard." He pressed a button on his gauntlet. "All Lemurian forces," he announced to the soldiers on the field, "move to the west as quickly as possible. The mountain is unstable. Move to the west. Double time!"

The forces began to run pell-mell to the west. The Fallen forces had all abandoned their posts and boarded their ships in haste. Soon, most Fallen were clear of the area. Lemurian troops continued to run, trying to get as much distance between them and the mountain.

Osiris, Charlotte, and Ronin tried to usher all the stragglers and aide those who were unable to move quickly. The ground shook and, in an instant, a gorge opened up in the ground behind them. Blasts of steam and heat escaped the earth, sending the trio flying back. The volcano rumbled to life. Rivers of lava exploded out from the mountain, spraying large chunks of rock and debris everywhere. Ronin helped Charlotte up and Osiris stood shakily next to them. Their comrades were hundreds of yards away at that point, and they were putting greater distance from the mountain by the second. Osiris knew it was too late for them. The earth shook so violently, it was all they could do to stay upright. They struggled to run, but the ground shifted so much that they couldn't put more than two strides together. Ronin gathered Charlotte up in his arms, trying to shield her from the falling debris. Then, Osiris remembered. He hit a button on his gauntlet. In seconds, high above them, Osiris's Spartan flew down to them.

"We can all jump on the Spartan," Osiris yelled. All Ronin could do was nod and give a thumbs up. The Spartan was only yards away when another explosion suddenly rocked the ground. Billowing smoke enveloped them. The poisonous gases filled their lungs and they coughed for dear life. They were now on a small island of rock surrounded by the churning fire of magma. Osiris looked up and saw a wave of lava looming above them. Soon, it would be all over. Soon...

Silence came over them. Osiris opened his eyes and saw they were inside the lava. To be more precise, they were inside a bubble that was inside the lava. Ronin and Charlotte stood from their crouched position and stared in wonder. They could no longer feel the tremors of the earth. In fact, they were ascending, pulling out of the lava.

Osiris was so enamored with his surroundings that he failed to notice the two girls standing at the middle of the protective sphere. The Caster, Lilyana, had her arms spread wide creating another force barrier around them. She was chanting in the ancient Atlantean language.

"Good thing we stuck around, eh?" Jennavieve said with a smirk.

CHAPTER THIRTY-SIX

FATAL BLOW

The Leviathan's head swooped down for another meal, but Jack and Lara fired concentrated thruster bursts to stay out of the monster's reach. The rain and surging ocean had all but extinguished the flames on the Titan's weapon, making it less effective against the Orichalcum metal hull of the Leviathan.

Max and Alana buzzed around the massive head of the snake, firing all their weapons at their disposal. Like waves against the granite, their efforts simply rolled off without much damage.

The Titan jumped up for a power swing. The ax whizzed through the air; its trajectory on line for a killing blow to the monster's head. It shifted slightly to the right, rendering a potential final strike to nothing more than a glancing blow.

Because of the momentum, the Titan was off balance. The serpent took advantage of the Titan's momentary instability and slashed down with its massive jaw. Jack and Lara reacted quickly, positioning the head of the ax in front of them. The Leviathan bit down and the ax wedged in the open mouth of the monster. The Titan dropped to one knee as it struggled to hold on to the shaft of the ax. The Leviathan's mouth was only a few yards from the Titan's head.

Alana saw the opening. "Hold it as long as you can," she said to

Jack and Lara. "I can initiate a self destruct sequence on my Spartan. I'll fly it into the Levithan's mouth before it detonates. The blast might be enough to destroy it."

"Alana, but…" Max started.

"I'm going to eject right before I fly my mech into its mouth. Be ready to catch me," Alana interrupted.

Relieved, Max nodded. "Ok, you got it."

"Just give me a moment to start the self destruct…"

"Max…" Jack and Lara yelled.

The Leviathan fired its red beam.

It blasted the Titan's head clean off of its body.

"No…" Alana whispered.

"MOM! DAD!" Max screamed over the comm.

"MOM…" Max's voice caught in his throat. His eyes searched frantically for any sign that his parents were safe. That they were still in the fight. He saw nothing. Then, as he reached out with his mind, he found his answer. Just like he had on the battlefield with the Fallen soldiers, this time he felt the life-force of his parents fade away.

Their vibrancy, energy, love. Gone.

It was as if someone reached into his chest and ripped a piece of his soul out of him. Max felt suddenly hollow. As a small breath escaped his lips, he closed his eyes. He searched the energy all around him, refusing to believe what his heart already knew. Desperately, he looked for an inkling of the familiar glow of his parents. A presence that he only just recently got back. A gift so finite, so precious, but it was gone.

Echoes of his parents' voices played in his mind.

228

Family is the most important thing, Son.

Max, I will always protect you.

We'll always be with you.

Max inhaled sharply and opened his eyes. They were now crackling with pure white energy. The energy surrounded his body, pulsing and vibrating all around him. Heat of the energy began to melt the hull of the Spartan until it was an oozing mass of twisted metal that fell away from him into the ocean below.

Alana watched, wide-eyed, as Max floated high above the ocean. Max stretched his arms out wide and tendrils of energy from all around began to flow to him. The winds subsided and the ocean calmed as Max absorbed more of the energy. Max was tapped in to Earth itself. She fed him an unlimited supply of power and Max was ready to take it all.

The Leviathan reared back and chomped down on Max, completely engulfing him in its massive jaws. Energy still continued to flow to Max. Even the power of the Leviathan was slowly leeched away. The din of energy increased until Alana had to cover her ears. The blistering sound was at a fevered pitch. Then, instant silence. The energy flow subsided.

BOOM!

A massive explosion emanated from the Leviathan's maw. The energy released completely, disintegrated the head and upper torso of the giant serpent. Secondary explosions rocked the rest of the body of the Leviathan and soon it was nothing more than a smoldering ruin.

Alana's Spartan was thrown back from the concussion wave of the explosion, but she managed to maintain her altitude. She shielded her eyes. The sphere of blinding light seemed to linger unnaturally. The collected energy was still being spent. As the ball of light grew dimmer, Alana could see Max at the epicenter. His body was splayed out. Energy shot from his eyes and mouth.

Max curled up into a fetal position and the energy constricted back to Max, as if he were breathing it all back in. Max began to fall, his limp body tumbling in the wind as he hurtled towards the murky depths of the ocean.

EPILOGUE

Simon ripped the VR helmet off of his head. The Tablets of Destiny dropped out of his hands and clanged on his console. He was breathing deeply. His body began to shake and tremble.

"I didn't know his parents were in the mech," he whimpered.

Primus whirled Simon's chair around. "What?"

"They were there. When I fired the Leviathan's main weapon. At point blank."

"How do you know?" Primus asked almost hysterically.

"I could feel them. I could feel them die. I didn't know," he began to cry.

"What's happening to me?" He grabbed Primus's arm. "The Tablets, they connected us somehow. The Key. I felt his pain. His sorrow. Primus, what's happening to me?!"

> File 1125 Section 3 of 7 > Subject > Origins

> Upload complete.

> Augmented Uniform Guard 1496 > Powering down.

ACKNOWLEDGEMENTS

Thank you to all the people who have picked up my books and gave them a chance. This has been one of the most exhausting and enjoyable experiences of my life. Writing is my passion and I am blessed to be able to share it with all of you.

A huge thanks goes to my editors and production team. These books do not happen without you.

My family and friends. Thank you. I'm a fool most of the time and you deal with it gracefully; for that, I will be forever grateful.

Mom and Dad. Good job raising me. I turned out descent enough.

Jenn, Jenna, and Lily. My girls. I do all this for you. I hope these stories keep you company when I can't be there. I love you.

ABOUT THE AUTHOR

PERRY COVINGTON is the author of the *Origins* series, *The Caster Wars*, *The Watcher* series, and *The Littlest Ninja*. Perry is also a journalist, writing for numerous publications. His books are available through Think Kings Publishing, a group who endeavor to bring indie fictional works to the forefront of mainstream entertainment. He lives in Southern California with his beautiful wife, two amazing daughters, and a crazy dog named Ninja.

LEARN MORE ABOUT PERRY, HIS NOVELS, AND
UPCOMING RELEASES AND EVENTS!

www.perrycovington.com

www.ingramcontent.com/pod-product-compliance
Lightning Source LLC
Chambersburg PA
CBHW030918120626
46554CB00001B/199